"Do you want to be my friend?"

Abby leaned in and pressed her lips to the warm skin below Trevor's scruffy jaw. "With benefits?"

All Abby heard and felt was Trevor's groan as it rumbled from his throat, and he wrapped his fingers around the back of her head and pulled her to him. Their lips met with passionate fury. This kiss was more...*heated*. Like water sizzling on a hot pan, the months of sexual tension that had bubbled between them came boiling over as they grabbed at each other frantically and kissed against the door of her fridge.

Trevor's hands slid up and down her body, exploring her curves, pushing her clothing out of the way. His body was pressed against hers, sandwiching her between his hard, warm front and the cold of the fridge door.

"God, Abby," he muttered on a harsh exhalation, with a shake of his head.

She could feel the hard length of him pressed against her belly. Thankfully, he kissed her once again then brought his lips to her ear and whispered, "Where's your bedroom?"

Dear Reader,

In my Blaze debut, *In the Boss's Bed*, Abby and Trevor provide much needed advice and guidance to Maya and Jamie, their respective best friends. But in the course of writing the book, I kind of fell in love with Abby and Trevor. I knew almost immediately that I had to give them their own story.

Abby and Trevor became fast friends when Maya and Jamie moved to Las Vegas. Neither is looking for a romantic relationship, but when they decide to try a *friends with benefits* arrangement, they think that they can maintain emotional distance while enjoying some wild nights together. But they soon find themselves way over their heads when their feelings enter the picture.

Friends-to-lovers is one of my favorite tropes, because why wouldn't somebody fall in love with their best friend? Who else knows your good and bad sides? Who knows what you like and what you don't? Who do you go to when you're having a bad day? But as we learn with Abby and Trevor, things aren't always that easy.

I hope you enjoy reading *In Her Best Friend's Bed*. If you ever want to chat, send me an email: jmargotcritch@gmail.com, or hit me up on Twitter: @juanitamcritch.

Cheers!

J

J. Margot Critch

In Her Best Friend's Bed

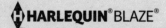

Recycling programs
for this product may
not exist in your area.

ISBN-13: 978-0-373-79956-5

In Her Best Friend's Bed

Copyright © 2017 by Juanita Margot Critch

Printed in U.S.A.

HARLEQUIN®
www.Harlequin.com

A12006 739305

Juanita Margot Critch currently lives in St. John's, Newfoundland, with her husband, Brian, and their two little buddies, Simon and Chibs. She spends equal amounts of time writing, listening to Jimmy Buffett's music and looking out at the ocean, all the while trying to decide if she wants coffee or a margarita.

Books by J. Margot Critch

Harlequin Blaze

In the Boss's Bed

As always, to Brian. Thank you for being the man all romance heroes aspire to be.

To lovely editor-extraordinaire Johanna Raisanen at Harlequin Blaze. Thank you for all of your guidance, support and patience. None of this could have happened without you.

1

TREVOR JONES LOOKED around the lounge of Swerve Las Vegas Hotel and Night Club, and as he sipped his champagne, one thing was clear—Jamie Sellers sure knew how to throw one hell of a party. He caught sight of his friend and Jamie's new fiancée, Maya, as they made their rounds, greeting people, shaking hands, hugging. Jamie was smiling, relaxed.

In all of the years that Trevor had known Jamie, he had never seen his friend look quite so laid-back. Trevor knew that normally this type of event, the opening of a new Swerve location, would have tied Jamie into a ball of frayed nerves. But Maya's presence and her love must have calmed him that evening. She had turned Jamie into a new man entirely. Of course, Trevor was happy for his friend. And he was proud of Jamie's accomplishments, but with his recent success in Las Vegas and the hand of his love, Trevor couldn't help but think that he and Jamie were about to spend *a lot* more time apart, and, as a grown man, that filled him with more gloom than he would have expected. Maybe Jamie's success, professionally and personally, made Trevor realize that he, himself, wasn't getting any younger. He was in his thirties. Maybe it was time for Trevor to move on with his life, settle down.

Trevor took a deep breath, inserted a finger under the collar of his shirt and pulled the constricting material away from his neck. He rolled his shoulders. The tailored jacket that had fit him perfectly earlier that evening now stretched across his shoulders and didn't give an inch, as his internal temperature rose high enough to boil water. Trevor couldn't wait to get back to his room to remove the suffocating layers.

He hated wearing suits.

Trevor's wardrobe normally consisted of casual wear—jeans and T-shirts. His work behind the bar required him to be comfortable and unrestricted in his movements, especially when it was time to do a little drink mixing and flair bartending to the *oohs* and *ahhs* of the crowd. But the second you fasten all of the buttons on a shirt up to the collar and add the silk noose of a necktie, a confining jacket and tight, shiny shoes, it was enough to make a man go crazy.

He took a gulp of champagne and a meaningful look at the hardworking staff behind the bar. He wished he was back there, in his element, instead of a guest at the party. He just wasn't in the mood to socialize, and Trevor wondered if Jamie would mind if he left the party early and went back to his room.

"You're pretty quiet tonight over here by yourself." He heard her voice behind him, interrupting his reverie. He recognized the voice—smoky, breathy—and he knew who he would see when he turned. But he wasn't prepared for the visage she presented. Abby, Maya's best friend. She was the feisty, pixie-haired blonde he had met on a couple of previous occasions before offering her a job behind the bar with him at the original Swerve, back home in Montreal.

He'd seen her earlier that night, in Jamie's office, when they had all privately celebrated the opening and the engagement of their friends before hitting the party. But, like him, she had since changed out of her casual clothing into something more appropriate for the opulent gathering. Tonight her short blond hair was gelled back, and she was wearing a long-sleeved black dress, the neckline high, swathing her collarbone. He would have considered it to be far too conservative for the woman whose fashion choices leaned toward daring or risqué, but he had just seen the back, which was cut to just above her perfect behind, and the slit in the leg that parted high on her thigh when she walked.

She had great legs, in addition to every other feature, and he knew she had a flawless body under all that dress, as he'd gotten more than a few glimpses at a pool party that Jamie had thrown months earlier. When his eyes returned to her face, her smile let him know that she had caught him checking her out. She pursed her lips at him and took a drink from her champagne flute. "I would've expected you to have at least two women on your arm by now."

With a cool smile, Trevor leaned in to her, close enough to smell her perfume, mingling with the smell of the champagne that lingered on her lips. "Oh, you know, I'm scoping the place out, weighing my options. How about you? No men here catching your eye?"

She laughed. The soft, raspy sound made him smile. She took a look around, surveying the room, and nodded appreciatively. "No one yet, but the night is young. There are lots of beautiful people here tonight."

"There certainly are," he answered, not able to take his eyes from her. *What other people?* If Trevor was being completely honest, he would admit that he hadn't actually noticed any of them, especially with Abby standing in front of him in one of the sexiest dresses he'd ever seen. "And what about your boyfriend?" Trevor asked her, eyebrow raised. "Luther, is it?"

"Luke," she corrected him with a side-eye glance. "And he's neither a Luther nor my boyfriend."

"Oh, really? What happened?" He tried his best to sound like the concerned friend he should be, all the while attempting to conceal his smile. Trevor never liked the guy; he wasn't good enough for a woman like Abby.

Abby rolled her eyes. "He used the *L* word."

"Loan?"

"Love," she said with a laugh, pushing his shoulder playfully.

"It's a bit soon for that, isn't it?" Trevor asked. "You guys weren't together very long."

"You are correct. We were together for five weeks."

"And the *L* word came out? Like, in conversation, or in the throes of passion?"

Abby giggled. "In a text message. This morning. Not one ounce of passion involved."

"So, what happened then?"

"I texted him back, saying that maybe we should see other people, and I went back to eating my crepes."

"That's cold."

Abby shrugged. "I'm not looking to be stuck in some relationship. Never have, never will. And he knew that." She shrugged. Clearly not too broken up about her recent breakup. She turned back to Trevor. "Look at us, just a couple of kids from Montreal, partying with the upper echelon of the Las Vegas elite." She smiled. But Trevor could tell that the curve of her lips was forced, and in her eyes was a look as weary as the one in his own.

"We sure are," he agreed, but his sigh was heavy. "It's a good time."

Abby's eyes were sharp as he felt their scrutiny, and it was a few seconds before she said anything. "Then why does it look like you're about to bolt out of here?"

She had him there. Instead of answering her, Trevor brought his champagne flute to his lips and regrettably found it empty. He wished for more in an effort to cool his internal temperature and to quench his too-dry throat. He looked at Abby's hand and noticed that she had drained her glass, as well. Turning, he gestured to the bar. "Care for another drink?"

"Sure."

He looked around, searching for a waiter with a tray of champagne, but he found none nearby. Figuring they could probably get their glasses quickly refilled at the bar, Trevor moved aside so she could go first. He instinctively placed an escorting hand at the small of her back, and his palm tingled at the connection with her smooth skin, exposed by the indecently low cut of the back of her dress and slightly chilled from exposure to the room's air-conditioning.

When he touched her, she stopped walking and looked up at him, her lips parted in surprise. Despite the considerable height provided to her by her stilettos, she was petite and the top of her head still only came to his chin. Trevor lowered his gaze to her red lips and found it nearly impossible to look elsewhere, until he forced himself and his eyes found hers. A beat of silence fell over them. Trevor could hear neither the music piping throughout the club nor the revelry of his fellow partygoers. He heard only the sound of his own heartbeat, pounding in his chest, and the blood rushing past his ears. And, for a moment, neither he nor Abby moved. Both of them seemed transfixed by the way his hand felt on her, how his palm flattened and molded to the smooth arch of her lower back.

Unable to tear his eyes from her, he took a chance. Testing the boundaries of both of them, Trevor moved his hand a little lower, his pinkie finger skimming the top of the material that curved over her behind. He watched Abby's shoulders rise and felt her ragged shudder when they fell again. He realized then that he had been holding his breath and he let it go, exhaling roughly.

Abby blinked and finally looked around the room. She opened her mouth a little farther as if to speak, and the spell broke. "Uh…how about that drink?"

Trevor pulled his hand away and fastened the buttons of his jacket hastily, leaving only the bottom one undone. Thankfully, the length of his jacket covered the makings of the erection that resulted from only touching her bare skin. He took a step back and extended a hand in the direction of the bar. "After you."

Abby nodded and walked ahead of him, with him staying a couple of steps behind her, and he couldn't help but notice the sexy sway of her hips under the dark color of her dress and the way its low back threatened to reveal more with every step she took.

They found two empty seats at the bar. The bartender was quick and in seconds they had fresh glasses of champagne in their hands. Trevor took a sip and hummed appreciatively. Of course the champagne was top-shelf. Jamie knew the importance of creating a good impression with his guests, and he would never skimp when it came to getting the good stuff. He watched the bar staff whom he'd helped hire and train as they worked quickly and efficiently together. He smiled. He was glad that they turned out to be a good team. If the party and grand opening of Swerve Las Vegas was any indication, Jamie was about to have yet another successful venture on his hands.

"Quite a shindig, eh?" Abby remarked as she drank her champagne, her eyes looking everywhere but at him. Trevor wondered if he had previously misread her. He feared that he had made her nervous, and in turn made things awkward between them, ruining the budding friendship that they'd formed.

"Yeah," he said with a smile. "Classic Jamie. The man knows how to show people a good time." He once again spied Jamie and Maya in the crowd as a couple of men shook Jamie's hand and shifted away, leaving the couple alone for once.

"Isn't it crazy that they're engaged?" Abby asked him. She was watching them as Jamie scooped Maya up in a bear hug, lifting her off her feet and kissing her. Abby smiled, obviously as happy for them as Trevor was. "It's so fast!"

"It certainly is. But they're good for each other. I'm glad it worked out for them," Trevor agreed, recalling the rocky road that had brought Jamie and Maya to that moment. "And I'm willing to bet that Jamie would like nothing more than for the both of them to get out of here and celebrate in private."

"You're telling me," Abby said with a laugh.

Trevor and Abby sat in silence for a bit, both watching the crowd of people swarming and mingling before them. Then Trevor surreptitiously glanced at the gorgeous woman beside him, and he considered his physical reaction to simply touching Abby. He'd been with his share of women and had certainly touched more than a bare back in his day, but when he was near Abby, it felt like something inside him shifted. Sure, he was attracted to her—*she's a beautiful woman*—but there was something else, something intangible that pulled at every fiber of his being, of his desire, when she was around.

He heard Abby laugh at something the bartender said to her. He frowned, feeling a small tinge of jealousy. But he shook his head to dispel it. It was never going to happen. It wouldn't be appropriate. The time for them to get together had long passed.

When Trevor had first met Abby, she was a customer at Swerve. He'd thought she was hot, but he didn't date customers. The next time they had met was at Jamie's pool party back in June. Abby had worn the smallest bikini and it still fueled many of his hottest fantasies.

Fast forward to the present, and Trevor's gaze drifted down to where she crossed her legs on the bar stool. The high slit of her skirt had fallen open, fully exposing her long, tanned and shapely legs. In his mind's eye, Trevor pictured himself kissing his way up those legs, starting at her delicate ankle, dragging his tongue along the toned muscle of her calf, nibbling her inner thigh as he rose over her...

"So, do you have any plans for later, or do you just want to sit here and stare at my legs all night?"

Busted. He looked at her face and smiled broadly, unembarrassed. She had caught him checking her out once again. He clearly wasn't being covert this evening. He must be off his game. Trevor laughed, and he had to think quickly. "Well, ah, I was just admiring your shoes. They're great, but I'm not sure how you can walk in those things."

She looked to her feet and the dangerously high heels. "If you like them so much, maybe you'll get a pair of your own at the Swerve holiday gift exchange," she told him pointedly.

She had him there. His libido came crashing back to earth when he finally remembered that she was his employee. When he'd heard that she was having trouble landing a job after graduating last spring, Trevor had hired Abby to work at Swerve and she had proved to be quite a valuable asset. Abby was an efficient, hard worker, and she kept the bar clean and tidy and the customers happy. He knew she wouldn't be with him for long, since it would only be a matter of time until her job search rewarded her with a career suitable to her qualifications. But hiring her had still been a great decision.

When he didn't reply, Abby laughed and sipped her drink. He noticed the flush on her cheeks. "I think I need a little air," she announced, facing him. She stood. "Care to join me?"

Trevor decided then that he would go anywhere with her. "Sure." When she started to make her way to the patio, he stopped her. "Wait. Have you seen the VIP rooftop bar in this place?"

Her eyes widened and she shook her head. "I have not. I didn't even know there was one. But I guess I shouldn't be surprised."

"Well, it's not officially finished yet, but Jamie showed me yesterday. It's great."

She looked around the room. "Where is it?"

"On the roof," he supplied with a smirk.

"You're such a smart-ass," she muttered, throwing a light punch on his shoulder. "How do we get there?"

"Come on, I'll show you."

He stood, careful to not touch her in any way, lest he lose control and throw her over his shoulder, run upstairs with her and lock them both in his room. They walked out of the club and past the regular bank of elevators to the one that would take them to the penthouse suites. From his pocket, Trevor removed the key card that Jamie had given him, emblazoned in gold with the letters *VIP*, and he inserted it into the slot to call the elevator.

"*VIP*, eh?" Abby asked him in a playful tone.

"Don't be too impressed," he told her as they stepped inside the elevator car. "It's only because I'm *very important*," he assured her, his voice deadpan, as he pushed the button to bring them to the rooftop.

Abby laughed, the soft, breathy sound filling the inside of the small elevator as it began its ascent.

Trevor watched her in the mirrored glass that covered the interior. Abby, however, was watching the numbers as they quickly climbed the floors to the top, but when she looked at the mirror and saw him staring at her, their reflections locked eyes. The only noise beside their breaths was the chime as the elevator announced that they had reached the rooftop.

The elevator doors pulled apart, revealing the open rooftop bar. Trevor could picture all of the people who would flock to Swerve just for the opportunity to be seen here and take in the view. He escorted Abby over to a high railing on the far side. The 360-degree view of the lights of the Las Vegas Strip, and of downtown in the distance, took his breath away. So far he had only seen the bar in the daylight. He was impressed then, but at night it was spectacular. The white leather furniture they walked past was sleek and crisp. And the dance floor, which would soon be filled with bodies moving to pulsing beats, was elevated and would be lit from below. He could only imagine the rush that would accompany dancing so high above the streets of one of the world's hottest party spots.

Trevor and Abby stopped at the railing and neither spoke as they took in the view. They could see the people and the revelers milling about below, but, being so high up, they could hear nothing in the silence of the empty rooftop. Despite the fact that they were in Las Vegas, the late-fall air at night held a slight chill, and he saw the small bumps rise on the skin of Abby's back. He shrugged off his jacket and placed it over her shoulders.

She pulled it closed over her chest. "Thanks." She hesitated. "I don't think I ever thanked you for letting me work at the bar. I really appreciate it."

"The pleasure is all mine," he said with a shake of his head. Her features were highlighted by the glow of the moon. She looked beautiful. "Any luck on the job front?"

She shook her head. "Big, fat goose egg," she told him, making an O with her thumb and forefinger. "I've got résumés out, had a couple of interviews, but nada."

"You'll find something," he assured her. He knew it was true, and it made him sad that he would soon be without her. "I know you won't be working with me forever, but it's nice to have you there. You're a natural behind the bar."

"Yeah, I can really pour a drink with the best of them," she scoffed.

Trevor frowned at her tone. He knew that she didn't take the job as seriously as she would the marketing career she dreamed of. He wished that she understood that bartending wasn't just about pouring beer and twirling a cocktail shaker. To be successful, one had to possess an innate quality that few people could claim to have. Most people could be *good* at bartending. But one had to be kind, personable, tough, funny, organized, dexterous and quick in order to be *great*. And she was. Abby's quick dismissal of the profession cut him to the quick and, even though he managed one of the hippest and most successful clubs in Montreal, it made him feel like a glorified bar boy.

"Hey, are you okay over there?" she asked him, breaking into his thoughts. "I don't think I've ever seen you this quiet or contemplative."

"Yeah, sure." He shook his head, dispelling the melancholy that had overtaken him. His smile was smooth. "I like your dress."

Abby looked down at herself and smoothed a hand down her front, over her flat stomach. Trevor's eyes followed it intensely. "This old thing?" she laughed.

"With the back, and the slit, I thought it might be a bit too much for tonight."

"Anything goes in Vegas," he offered with a smile.

"It sure does. What's the old saying? 'What happens in Vegas—'"

"'Stays in Vegas.' Yeah," he finished for her and trailed off. They watched the lights and the action on the street below them. He heard her dress rustle and he felt her shift closer to him, until they were touching, side by side. He looked at his hands grasping the railing, and he saw her fingers slide across it, creeping until they touched his. The same electric current he'd felt earlier, when he'd had his hand on her back, jolted from her fingers to his.

He turned away from the railing to face her, and he brought his hand to rest lightly on her hip, ushering her closer to him, until they were almost pressed together. Her breasts grazed his chest and he tensed, his hand roamed under the jacket to settle once again on her bare lower back. This time, he wasn't about to pull away from her. He looked down at Abby, unable to take his eyes away from her parted lips. He wanted to kiss her more than anything.

Trevor heard nothing but the faint notes of music that flittered up to them from below. He leaned in and brought his lips to hers, barely skimming them, just enough to get the smallest taste, but Trevor wanted more, and he took her bottom lip between his own, and he barely heard it when someone called out to him. He jerked back quickly, away from Abby, and they turned to the newcomer. Trevor cursed when he saw that it was Jamie, whose hand was tightly clasped in Maya's.

"There you guys are," he said and turned to Trevor. "I should have known I'd find you up here."

"And you did," Trevor responded. It seemed Jamie was oblivious to what they had interrupted, but one look at Maya's raised eyebrow told him that she didn't miss much. "What's up?"

Jamie's smile was sheepish. "I, uh, just wanted to show Maya the view up here at night."

Trevor laughed. "Sure." He was skeptical that the view was the only thing Jamie wanted to show Maya. "It really is something else, though."

Jamie chuckled at Trevor's doubt, clapped his palm on Trevor's shoulder. "Sorry we haven't been able to talk all night, man. Lots of hands to shake."

"No problem," Trever said. "I get it. It's been a crazy night for you. How are you holding up?"

"Honestly, I'm exhausted," Jamie replied, dragging a hand through his dark hair. He threw a glance at Maya. "We might take off."

"You're leaving your own party?" Abby asked.

"Yeah, I've already spoken to everyone I needed to," Jamie explained. "We need to hit the sack. It's been a big day."

"And I repeat—sure…" Trevor smirked at his friend. He knew Jamie was going to bed with his new fiancée, but he doubted that either of them would be getting much sleep.

"It's been a long day," Maya concurred, unable to pry her eyes away from Jamie's face.

Abby nodded, clearly unconvinced, as well. "Uh-huh."

"You both suck," Jamie said, laughing and looking back and forth between Trevor and Abby. "Anyway, we're leaving. But would you guys like to get breakfast tomorrow morning before your flight home?"

"Yeah, sure." Trevor nodded. "Sounds good to me."

"Me, too," Abby responded.

"Great. Let's meet at the café here in the hotel. Around eleven o'clock?"

Trevor and Abby both nodded in agreement, and they watched as Maya pulled Jamie away from them, into the elevator and most definitely down to their penthouse suite. Before Trevor knew it, he and Abby were once again alone.

Abby was first to speak. She exhaled a breath. "You know, I should be getting to bed, too." She let out a yawn that Trevor knew was forced. But he walked her to the elevator and they waited for the car that would take them down.

When they got to the main floor, he escorted her to the elevators that would bring them to the guest rooms. Trevor stopped Abby before she got into an elevator alone. "Want me to walk you up?" he asked her. His intentions were mostly those of a complete gentleman, who wished to see her to her room safely. But part of him was hopeful that she would invite him into her room so that they could finish what they'd started.

She shook her head, dashing his hopes. "No. It's not necessary. I'm a big girl."

Trevor didn't want to push it. He knew that Abby was a strong woman. She didn't need or want a man to look after her. If he insisted on walking her to her door, it would just make her angry. "Even so. Sure you don't need the company?"

"I'm sure. I'll be fine." She smiled at him. "Thank you."

"Why don't you text me when you get up there, though? Just so I know you made it all right."

"Fine," she said, laughing as she walked into the elevator. "See you in the morning."

The doors closed between them, and Trevor was all alone in the lobby. He sighed and downed the rest of his champagne, emptying the glass he still held in his hand. He walked back into the club. The party was still in full swing and he surveyed the room full of strangers. He figured he might as well head up to his room. He and Abby had to fly back to Montreal the next afternoon, and shortly after landing, he would have to head to the club for some meetings that he'd scheduled with a couple of vendors, and he had to finish the staff schedule for the upcoming week and input the end-of-month inventory numbers, and he had to make arrangements for upcoming holiday events booked at the club... His to-do list was a mile long.

On the other hand, he knew that it would be a while before he'd be in Vegas again, so he might as well enjoy the party and the free drinks and the glamourous company while he could. He was never one to turn down a good party. "I can sleep on the plane," he muttered with a shrug.

He really wished that Abby had stuck around. He missed her. She was great to talk to. They had become such good friends in the past couple of months. It turned out that they had a lot in common and enjoyed each other's company. They went to movies together, had dinner together, talked through their respective problems—Abby would even confide in him about the men in her life.

Alone, he walked back to the bar and ordered another drink. He sat at an empty stool and turned around to once again survey the room, thinking about Abby back in her room, and how he wished he was up there with her, but she'd rebuffed his offer. And he took that as a definite sign that she was interested in nothing more than friendship with the likes of him.

"Is this seat taken?"

Trevor turned his head to the voice and smiled when he saw a gorgeous woman in a short red dress standing beside the empty stool next to him. He held out a hand, gesturing to the stool. "It's all yours."

ABBY TAPPED HER foot as she waited for the elevator to take her to her floor. She folded her arms and realized that she was still wearing Trevor's jacket. She pulled the collar to her nose and inhaled his scent as it completely enrobed her. She could still feel the tingle of his lips on hers. And she knew that if one brush of his mouth against hers had elicited such a reaction, why hadn't she asked Trevor to come up with her? He'd offered. But for some reason she'd said no. Was it fear? If she had invited him up, then their friendship would have been irrevocably changed, and his friendship was too valuable to her. *But, God*, she shivered at the thought, *what a night it would be*.

Abby took out her phone and saw the many messages from Luke. She sighed and walked out of the elevator when the doors pulled apart at her floor, heading for her room, but she paused outside her door. Luke had broken her first rule. *Don't get serious*. She didn't want a serious relationship. Just a little bit of fun. She turned her head and looked longingly at the door she knew belonged to Trevor's room. He was still down there at the party and she could have been, as well. She checked her watch and, with a sigh, she realized that it was still pathetically early. Determined, Abby turned on her heel and walked back to the elevator.

Before she could change her mind, the doors opened and she stepped back inside the same elevator she had just vacated and drummed her fingers against her thigh as she counted the numbers as she descended to the lobby. Maybe she and Trevor could continue the kiss they'd shared. Maybe more.

When she got back to the nightclub, the party was still in full swing, the lights had dimmed and the music had gotten louder. More people were dancing. Abby squinted into the crowd, scanning the room for the familiar face that she sought. But it was his laugh that she somehow heard over the din of the club before she could pick him out of the crowd. He was sitting at the bar. She smiled and started to walk to him. She was almost there when she stopped short and ducked behind a couple of men enjoying themselves nearby. When she got around them, she had a clear view of the bar.

And next to Trevor was a woman. A glamorous brunette in a short dress on the bar stool next to him. Trevor smiled at her. Abby's mouth dropped in shock, outrage or maybe disappointment. Trevor had just been kissing her on the rooftop, and here, just minutes afterward, he sat, obviously making up for lost time, drinking with another woman.

Disappointment and anger roiling through her system, Abby exhaled and left the club. She pushed the call button for the elevator several times. Coming after him had been a mistake. One she wouldn't make again. She might not be looking for a relationship, but she also couldn't get involved with a man like Trevor. She was glad she'd seen him because, even though she would still count him as a friend, she now knew exactly what type of guy Trevor Jones was. And it was all she needed to affirm her decision to stay away from men in general. Whether they were quick to fall in love or they were players, it was best for her to stay away from all of them.

2

Three months later...

"WHAT CAN I get you?" Abby leaned over the bar to hear the order of a heavily made-up woman over the pounding music. Swerve was packed that night and the music was loud and driving. Wednesday nights were never usually so busy. But semester break had started and the college students were out en masse.

The woman, definitely past college age by a number of years, pursed her red lips. "Can I get two screaming orgasm shots?"

Abby had no idea what the woman was talking about.

She racked her brain for whatever a screaming orgasm shot could be, and she pulled out her phone to look up the recipe, but when she looked over at Trevor, who was busy filling his own orders, and realized that she had the opportunity to have a little fun with him.

"Hey, Trev," she called across the bar. "Think you can give this lady a couple of screaming orgasms?"

Trevor smirked and finished his own drinks before

sauntering over to her. "I think I can handle that." He grinned. "Wouldn't be the first time it's happened."

Abby rolled her eyes and walked away. Of course the blonde wearing all that makeup was most definitely Trevor's type. And even though she basically served the woman up to Trevor, Abby couldn't help but feel a small wrench of something—hurt? Jealousy?—in the pit of her stomach as she watched Trevor flirt with her. It was a feeling she hadn't experienced since Vegas, seeing Trevor with that other woman at the bar, just after they'd kissed. Abby had never told him that she'd come back to the bar three months ago and seen him with that woman.

And now it was too late. Their relationship had long transcended potentially romantic to become strictly platonic. Sure, they were flirty and frequently peppered their conversation with naughty double entendres, but they were friends, and, with Maya living in Las Vegas, Abby greatly appreciated having a good friend, even if he was definitely *not* the type of guy she was going to date...if she was ever going to date anyone again.

Which she wasn't.

But being friends hadn't stopped her from still feeling his lips on hers, and the promise of more that flowed from just a simple graze of their lips, the heat of his hand on her bare back...

Abby looked up. She was still in Swerve. Still in Montreal, not on top of the roof of Swerve's Las Vegas location; meanwhile, dozens of thirsty patrons lined her bar. She couldn't afford to be distracted by some guy, hunky sexpot, or not. She had to regain her focus. She had to concentrate on herself, getting her career back on track and not let herself get distracted by men, the ones who wanted a commitment or guys like Trevor. Bad boys. Players. She shook her head and got back to work.

Abby reached into the cooler and took out a couple of beer bottles. She popped off the tops and passed them to a man who was trying to catch her eye. She ignored his advances and continued on to the next customer. She cast another quick glance at Trevor, just as he turned his head and caught her looking at him. He pulled away from the woman, moving to fill other drink orders. But the woman called out to him again and reached out, grabbing his forearm, her long red nails grazing the dark ink that covered it. She handed him her card and Abby was surprised that the woman didn't kiss it first, to leave a print of her red lipstick on it. Trevor smiled and pocketed it.

And another notch on the bedpost...

Why did she care?

When Trevor continued his work, Abby watched the woman walk away, carrying her shot glasses to a friend at a nearby table. Trevor passed behind Abby, the hard muscles of his chest grazing her back as he side-stepped around her in the tight space. She could feel his heat through the material of both their shirts. He mumbled a soft, awkward apology near her ear, his warm breath rippling over her, the deep timbre of his murmur rattling around in her brain. She had to force herself to shake away the wave of desire that passed through her body. There was nothing remotely romantic about the contact. They were sharing limited space behind the bar, and they bumped together or brushed past each other on a nightly basis. This time should have been no different.

But tell that to her now-moist panties…

Abby went about her work, making drinks for thirsty patrons. A customer ordered two margaritas on the rocks, with salt. Abby nodded her approval, looking for the ingredients. She picked up a bottle of tequila and grabbed the lime juice. She wet the rims of the glasses with a lime wedge and dunked them in a dish of coarse salt. Abby loved a good margarita and wished that she was on the other side of the bar ordering it, instead of the person making it. She looked at the bottles in front of her and realized one was missing. She went to the backup bottles of liqueur to find another, but found none.

"Trevor, where's the extra Cointreau?" she called without looking at him.

"Try the cupboard below the glassware," he suggested.

Abby bent at the waist and checked the shelves. Trevor was right—it was exactly where he'd said it would be. She stood and turned to face him and he quickly looked away, as if she'd caught him checking her out. It wouldn't have been the first time.

She glanced around the crowded bar. Bartending wasn't exactly what she'd envisioned her career would be after graduation. Thankfully, Trevor had offered her a job at Swerve. But as her feet ached in the heels she insisted on wearing—*they make my legs look great with this skirt*—she thought about the dozens of applications for marketing positions she'd submitted around the city and hoped that she would hear something promising soon. She had an interview the next morning. Maybe it would be the one that got her out from behind the bar, where Trevor distracted her at every turn with accidental physical contact, the smell of his cologne, his dark chuckle when he laughed…

She paused for a moment and watched Trevor at work, his masterful, strong hands as he made drinks. He tossed a vodka bottle behind his back with one hand and then, with the other, he reached for a cocktail shaker and twirled it, as well, before catching it. The man was good. He was in complete control. He was built for that type of work, and the awards and accolades he'd won were well earned.

Abby's focus returned to those hands, though—his long fingers, the soft, dark hair covering corded wrists that flexed with every movement, the collage of black ink that snaked up his forearms, starting at his wrists and disappearing under the material of his black shirt that he'd rolled up to his elbows. She imagined him doing other things with those hands. Hot things. Sexy things. To her. Running them up and down her body until she cried out…

Abby blinked out of her fantasy. *God, focus.* She and Trevor were coworkers and friends. That was it. Whatever could have happened between them romantically, *that kiss*, was in the past. The moment was over. She glanced up and saw the blonde woman standing with a friend at a nearby table. She waved a perfectly manicured hand at Trevor and Abby saw him smile and wink back at the woman. She sighed and moved on to the next customer, as she remembered her resolve to not fall under the spell of a man. She could do better, live for herself and no one else, not like Screaming Orgasm Lady or even her own mother.

She put all sexy thoughts of Trevor out of her head, and she got back to what he was paying her to do.

3

THE NEXT AFTERNOON, Abby pulled into the empty parking lot of Swerve. She was running late, having just come from her job interview. She thought that it went well, and her hopes were high. Still wearing her suit, she crossed the parking lot. Inside the club, Abby started for the ladies' restroom, so she could change into her miniskirt and official Swerve tank top. But she stopped. The bathroom was located at the other end of the club. She was already late for her shift, and any minute she could spare getting ready would be great. So instead of heading down to the restroom, she ducked into Trevor's office and shut the door behind her. He wouldn't mind. Hell, she could go in, change and be out prepping the bar before he even showed up. If he showed up on time.

He probably won't be if he went home with that blonde tart last night. Maybe she had herself a couple more screaming orgasms, Abby thought with a bitter grimace as she pulled off her blazer. She'd noticed the woman hanging around for the rest of the night, never taking her eyes from Trevor. And when they had walked out, locking up the bar, the blonde had been waiting for him in the parking lot. Not wanting to stick around to see the obvious outcome, Abby gave Trevor a brief, friendly fist bump and then they'd parted ways.

"Okay, that wasn't fair," she chastised herself as she unbuttoned her blouse. "Both he and the incredible Screaming Orgasm Lady are adults. Maybe the only things screaming were her pores under all that makeup." *Heh.*

"That wasn't fair, either," she muttered, trying to convince herself. "They can do whatever they want." And she wasn't about to blame a woman who might have Trevor all to herself for a night. Just because Abby had passed up the opportunity to spend what would have been an unbelievable night with him, it didn't mean that any other sane woman in the world would do the same thing.

TREVOR PARKED HIS car next to Abby's in the Swerve parking lot. It was March and the chill of winter still hung in the air. He wished spring would come soon, as he was looking forward to getting his motorcycle back out on the road. His car was nice enough, but driving it paled in comparison to taking a bike out on the open road. He unbuckled his seat belt and yawned, rubbing his fingers over his eyes. He was beat. He'd been at the club until three that morning, and he was even later getting home than usual, after waiting for the cab he'd called to pick up the blonde woman who'd been flirting with him all night. He remembered the weary sigh he'd given when he saw her standing outside the door, looking for him. She had been persistent, but he'd sent her on her way.

Once home, he'd had one hell of a time getting to sleep. After tossing and turning in his bed, he'd considered it useless, poured himself a double scotch and collapsed in front of his television, and it was daylight before he felt his eyes drift closed in surrender. Physically, he was in great shape, but a busy night at the bar now seemed to take more out of him than it used to. When he was in his twenties, he could work all night and still have the energy to party until daylight. But lately the aches in his feet, wrists and joints were more pronounced, as was the weariness of his mind, and he wondered how much longer he would be able to keep up with the pace.

But it wasn't the hard work or even the blonde woman who had waited for him outside the club that kept his mind racing in the early hours of this morning. It was Abby Shaw. Every time he had closed his eyes she was there, her long legs, short blond hair, bright smile, the feisty glint in her eye and certainly her shapely ass when she bent over to retrieve the liquor bottle—it was as if he had memorized her every feature. Since that night in Vegas when he'd kissed her, he couldn't get her out of his mind.

They hadn't even spoken of the night, the party at Jamie's hotel or even the city itself. It all reminded him that it was as telling a sign as any that she wasn't interested in pursuing any sort of relationship with him. Which was fine with him since he sure wasn't going to date one of his employees.

And then there was their friendship to consider. He didn't want to risk losing her. Although she was gorgeous and sexy and a lot of fun to hang out with, he saw what happened when Abby got scared and ran away from her boyfriends. She pushed them aside, usually because a man tried to get close to her. He knew there was something in her past that made her feel that way, but she'd never told him what it was. With how Trevor had been feeling lately, the weariness that accompanied his desire to settle down and act like an adult, he knew that either way, it wasn't in the cards for him and Abby to be any more than friends.

He scrubbed his stubbled jaw with his palm and realized that he'd forgotten to shave. *Great.* With one more yawn for good measure, Trevor reached into his pocket for his keys to the club and from the backseat pulled a case of top-shelf vodka. People went crazy for the stuff and didn't mind paying the exorbitant price for it. *To each their own.* Those customers paid his bills, and the tips cushioned his savings and investment accounts nicely. He hefted the case into his arms, made sure he had a good handle on it and headed to the club.

Inside, he grimaced at the glare of the lights. He pushed his sunglasses farther up his nose and walked to the stockroom to unload the box of liquor. He pulled one bottle out to put behind the bar and then headed back. Before he made it back to the bar, Trevor stopped at the closed door of his office. Strange. He didn't normally close it after checking out each night. He walked to the door, still holding the bottle, and pushed it open.

Surprised, Trevor dropped the bottle to the floor, and the frosted glass shattered into hundreds of liquor-soaked pieces. Abby stood in front of him, wearing nothing but her short black skirt and high heels. The smell of expensive vodka filled the air, as she clutched her black tank top in front of her stomach, and it took Trevor less than one second to focus on the wide expanse of smooth, alabaster skin of her high, full breasts and flat stomach. They stood in stunned silence for a couple of beats. Trevor was oblivious to everything but her, even the alcohol seeping into his sneakers.

It was a few moments before she broke free of her shock and came to her senses. "Oh, God, Trevor," she screeched and raised her arms to cover her perfect breasts. Trevor frowned briefly, mourning the loss of the view of her dusty-pink nipples.

"Oh, shit!" He became cognizant of the mess at his feet and bent to clean it up. "I'm sorry." He stared at the floor, trying to look away from her, attending to the glass. "I didn't even know you were in here." He raised his hand and turned his head slightly. "What are you doing in here?"

"I came in here to change out of my suit." In his periphery he could see her turn her back to him and pull her tank top over her head. "What are *you* doing here?"

"This is my office." When Trevor looked up a little, he caught her dark, distorted reflection in the screen of the turned-off computer monitor on his desk. He felt like a lecher, but he couldn't force his eyes away.

"But you're early," she protested. He watched her reflection as she straightened her shirt over her chest and down to her waist. And she huffed out a breath that made her breasts rise and then fall. "I'm done. You can turn around now."

Trevor did as she told him. She was fully dressed, stuffing her business suit into her duffel bag. She didn't look at him.

"I'm sorry," she said with an outward breath. "I shouldn't have used your office."

"It's fine. Use it anytime you want," he told her. "I'll

just knock when the door is closed. Who knows when there will be a half-naked woman in here?" He laughed.

"Knowing what I do about you, it really could happen at any time," she retorted, one eyebrow raised.

Trevor frowned at her approximation of him; nothing like that had ever happened to him at work. "I'm sorry if I embarrassed you. I really didn't know that you were in here."

Abby laughed and pushed past him. "You didn't embarrass me at all. I know I look good naked." She winked at him and walked behind the bar to start work.

Trevor exhaled roughly and watched her. He replayed her words in his brain: *I know I look good naked.*

Yeah, he thought. *No lie there.*

IT WAS A few hours later, and Abby ducked into the small backroom off the bar for a quick, much-needed break to sit down and drink some water. Her feet were sore—why did she always opt to wear heels to work? She rolled her ankles and pulled out her cell phone. On the screen she saw a notification of a missed call from a number that was only vaguely familiar to her. She dialed her voice mail. The mystery was soon solved when the message started playing, and she realized it was the voice of Michael Arnett, the man who had interviewed her earlier that day.

She turned the volume up on her phone, so she could hear over the din of the club. "Hello, Ms. Shaw," Arnett's voice on the recorded message sounded in her ear. "I'm just calling to let you know that we really enjoyed meeting you today…"

She smiled and sat straight. *This is it.*

"But we have decided to go in another direction with hiring for the position. We'll keep you in mind in the future. Good luck in your job search."

Abby disconnected the phone and slumped in her chair, huffing out a frustrated breath. She thought that she'd completely killed that interview, and to find out that she hadn't gotten the job—well, it sucked.

This night just keeps getting better and better...

Abby frowned and mentally checked off yet another opportunity that she'd missed. She glanced at her watch—just over four hours left before she could go home and wallow in self-pity. She might as well get back out there. She'd been away from the bar for five minutes, leaving Trevor on his own. She stood and opened the door, and she looked out at the bar. Trevor somehow managed to keep the place going on his own. He didn't really need her back there and she was certain he only offered her the job to be nice. She wasn't a great bartender and she felt she was in his way most of the time. But he never complained.

With a sigh, she walked behind the bar and plastered her biggest smile on her face—as phony as a three-dollar bill. She was bummed, but she wouldn't let it get in the way of doing her job. She might only be a bartender, but for now it was her job and she would do her best.

Trevor caught her eye and gave her a curious look, furrowing his brows at her. She shook her head, dismissing him. He watched her for a moment longer before returning to his work and letting her get on with hers.

WHEN LAST CALL sounded and all the patrons had stumbled out, Trevor took a deep breath, exhausted. They were busy, maybe even busier than they had been the night before. Spring break meant a bigger crush of new faces, in addition to loyal locals, in the bar. Financially, it was great. Jamie would be happy with the numbers and Trevor and Abby had both benefited as well, but they'd worked their asses off for their tips.

Trevor locked the door and watched Abby as she wet a blue cloth with sanitizer and started cleaning up. He knew that there was definitely something going on with her. Ever since she'd taken her break, her demeanor had changed. Sure, she was smiling, but he knew better. He knew it was fake. Something had upset her. But what?

"Everything okay over there?" he called out to her, approaching the bar.

"Yeah, fine," she responded, scrubbing a spot on the stainless steel without looking up.

Trevor wasn't at all convinced. He walked back to her, leaning against the bar. "Are you sure? It looks like something is bothering you."

"No," she started. "Well, yes." She threw down her rag. "I got a call about my interview this morning…"

"Really?" Trevor was interested. He hoped for a happy ending to her story, but, by the look on her face, he knew it was anything but.

"Yeah, I didn't get it. They went in another direction. HR speak for 'you suck and never come back.'"

He frowned. "You don't suck, Abby. I'm sorry."

"Thanks."

So that was it. She was disappointed that she hadn't gotten the job. Trevor wasn't looking forward to losing her, but he didn't like to see her beautiful smile faltering from frustration and disappointment. Trevor hated to see her upset. He reached into the beer cooler under the bar and withdrew two bottles. He popped the top off one and passed it to Abby.

She accepted it, raising an eyebrow. "Drinking on the job? That's not like you."

He shrugged and opened his own beer before he began wiping down the counters. "We had a crazy night here. I think we've earned it."

She nodded. "That's true. Thank you." She saluted him with the green bottle and took a long swallow.

He watched her meticulously tidy the counter behind her and arrange the liquor bottles, making sure they were located on the appropriate shelves and the spouts were clean. While the servers were responsible for making sure the rest of the club was clean, he and Abby concentrated on the bar and making sure the cash registers and the bank deposit balanced at the end of the night.

They cleaned side by side, not talking, both using extra force to scrub the surfaces, whether it was necessary or not. Trevor wondered if they were both taking out their frustration—sexual or otherwise—on the countertops. They cleaned and then recleaned. Trevor normally insisted on a spotless bar, but they were in danger of entirely wiping the chrome from the bar top.

The cocktail servers had all finished their own work and left by the time Trevor and Abby pulled away from the now-immaculate bar area. Trevor looked around and realized they were alone in the building.

Abby threw down her cloth and finally proclaimed their work done. She disposed of their empty beer bottles, and he watched her as she stretched to reach the bottles on the top shelf behind the bar. Trevor couldn't help but appreciate the length of her body, her shirt riding up to give him a peek at the smooth skin on her back, and he saw the top of the butterfly tattoo that he knew was there, just above her hip. He managed to somehow avert his eyes just in time as she turned around holding a bottle of expensive tequila and two shot glasses.

He looked at her bounty, eyebrow raised in question. She ignored him as she poured two shots. "I'm in need of something a little stronger than beer tonight," she explained. "What do you say?"

"Yeah, what the hell?" he said with a smile. He took the shot she offered before he turned back to the cash register and began counting the money.

Abby took her shot, as well, and then she glanced around the bar. He knew she was looking for something else to clean. "Why don't you go sit down?" he told her. "I just need a couple of minutes here." It was a rule that the staff always leave the club in groups at the end of the night. He didn't want any of them vulnerable late at night in the parking lot. Who knew what kind of drunks or weirdos were out there?

"Sure." Abby shrugged her shoulders and, taking the tequila bottle, she walked to a nearby table.

Trevor removed the money from the register and looked up briefly to see her pour another shot, a frown taking over her entire gorgeous face.

"You'll find something, Abby," he told her. Her eyes rose from her bottle to hit his directly, her gaze cutting a path straight to his belly. "Just keep at it. You're a catch. Any business would be lucky to have you. I know I am." A swell of melancholy rose in his chest, for her sadness and his own. He would miss her like crazy if she worked anywhere else.

"Does that mean I can use you as a reference?" she

asked with a mirthful smile, before raising the shot glass to her mouth and knocking back the tequila.

Trevor laughed, but the sound died as he watched the muscles in her delicate throat bounce as she swallowed the liquor. When she brought the glass down to the table, it hit with a heavy clink. How much time did he spend watching Abby while she looked absolutely sexy doing completely mundane things? "Pour me another?" he asked, shoving his glass across the bar. She did as he asked, and then she poured her own.

"You trying to get me drunk?"

"I would never think of it," he said with a wink. "Plus, I'm not the one pouring."

"Well, I can't let you drink alone," she explained carefully.

"How generous of you," he said, laughing, and lofted his shot glass. *"Sláinte,"* he said. He felt the second shot hit his belly, not as harsh as the first. But he was glad that she'd selected a smoother, higher-end tequila for their bingeing. Trevor didn't think he could handle the burn of a cheaper brand.

"What's that?"

"An Irish toast. A cheers to good health. My old man used to say it a lot before he took a drink."

"Sláinte," she repeated. "I like it."

"I'm pretty certain that neither of us can drive home now," he took a breath, the tequila starting to hit him in the pit of his empty stomach.

Abby shrugged as she sauntered back to her table. Trevor couldn't help but notice the sway of her hips under her short skirt. She threw a look over her shoulder. "I don't live far. I'll walk. And I'm not quite ready to head home to an empty apartment just yet. Plus, I'm having fun relaxing right here. It's been a long time since we've hung out."

"It has been far too long," Trevor agreed, closing the register with an authoritative slam. He finished with the cash duties by printing off the sales receipts and totaling the nightly deposit. He could officially call it another great night in the books, as he looked over the numbers. The bar was doing well in his capable hands, if he did say so himself.

He picked up a stack of bills and left the bar to sit with Abby at the booth. He cut the stack in half and passed over her share of the tips.

Abby took her money. "Nice. Thanks."

"Pretty good night, huh?"

Abby flicked through the stack of bills with her thumb. "It sure was."

"What are you going to do with your vast riches?" he asked her, joking, pocketing his own share.

"Well, I think I'm going to splurge on some grand luxuries." She sighed wistfully. "You know, things like electricity, cell phone bill—ooh, there's some really fancy bread and milk that I've been *dying* to try," she finished with a laugh.

Trevor laughed with her, but she worried him. He frowned. "Are you doing okay, financially? I can schedule you for more hours, or I can float you a loan, if you want."

She shook her head and put a hand on his arm. Her light touch made his heart stutter in his chest. "Trevor, I'm fine. It was just a joke. *Ha-ha.* Sure, it's a little harder to pay the rent with Maya gone. But I am fine. See?" She picked up the stack of bills in front of her and waved it in Trevor's face.

"Thanks to you, I've got a job where I make fat stacks of cash and I can drink for free." For emphasis she poured two more shots. After she swallowed, she giggled. "I'll be fine until I find a real job." She smacked a palm to her forehead. "Oh, shit, I'm sorry. I know this *is* your job. I didn't mean—"

"It's fine, Abby," he assured her, sweeping a hand through the air of the empty club. "All of this is my kingdom."

"You certainly get your pick of the ladies in the kingdom, that's for sure."

Trevor frowned again. He didn't normally use the club to pick up women. He never overserved them to make them bend to his will, and he never went for the college girls, who were always trying to get him in bed… And he *never* let his staff see him go home with a woman. He didn't want to set a bad example and have them to think it was okay or an acceptable business practice. But he wondered where she got the idea that he did.

"What are you talking about?" While he had been a bit wild in the past, he wasn't the *man whore* that she seemed to think he was. He hadn't even been with anyone in months. While Trevor didn't normally care what people thought of him, it stung that Abby had a negative opinion of him. What she thought mattered to him.

"You know," Abby said, with a slight slur. "That woman last night, that girl in Vegas…"

When Abby trailed off, Trevor was surprised. "What girl?" It was the first time either of them had mentioned their trip to Sin City.

"That girl at Jamie's party," she went on. "After we

parted ways, I went back to my room, you met her at the bar."

"You came back to the party?" Trevor narrowed his eyes at her. He barely remembered the woman who had sat beside him at the bar in Vegas.

"Yeah."

"Why?"

She scoffed. "Why does it matter? You were otherwise occupied."

"That's not how it was, Abby—" He wanted to clear the air, explain that he wasn't the complete horndog player that she apparently thought he was. "You've got the wrong idea. I didn't spend the night with her. I finished my drink and went to bed. Alone. And that woman last night? I called her a cab and waited here until she was in it."

"It's okay!" she insisted. "You're a guy. You have those typical male urges. And you're hot. I see how women look at you and how you talk to them. You're smooth. I'm surprised you don't have to beat the women off with a stick every night."

Trevor leaned back, away from her touch, and cleared his throat roughly around the lump that had formed there. Abby wasn't far off. He was often on the receiving end of female attention, but what he couldn't tell her was that, since that night in Vegas, he hadn't been interested in any other woman who came on to him. They were quiet for a moment. "So, any new fellows on the scene?" he asked her, hoping to steer the conversation away from himself.

Abby poured another shot, knocked it back and laughed bitterly. "No," she said. "There are *certainly* no fellows—new or otherwise—on the scene. Oh! I haven't told you, have I?"

"Told me what?"

"Well, after I ended things with Luke a few months back, I decided to give up men," she said, slamming her glass to the table with a loud thud.

"You're *giving up men*?" he asked. "What do you mean?"

"Exactly what I said. I'm no longer in the dating game."

"So, you're never going to date again?" He paused. "What about sex?" He crossed his arms, creating a safe distance between them.

She paused. "What about it?"

"Well," he said, his smile smug, "I can't be the only one with those *typical urges*. What are you going to do to fulfill those?"

"I didn't say that I was giving up *sex*." Abby rolled her eyes. "I'm just not going to be dating anymore. No more relationships."

"Okay." Trevor was still skeptical, but he was intrigued. "So, what exactly brought this about?"

"I'm glad you asked, Trevor. Let me tell you…" Her words ran together a little and he knew that they should go home, but he was having a great time. She held up her hand and grasped one finger in her other hand. "One—my tendency is to only go for these guys who want to settle down and get married immediately, and then expect me to have, like, twelve babies." She screwed up her face in a scowl. "You know that's not me. Never has been. And I always let them know where I stand on that. I tell them not to fall in love with me. I can't help it that they do." She stopped to take a breath.

Trevor knew she wasn't finished. "Then there's all the losers, bad boys, playboys. I don't want any more of those *boys*. There've been too many of those. So I decided that it's best to not see any of them."

"Okay," Trevor said carefully. "Makes sense. Anything else?"

"Why, yes, there is." Abby continued her list, grasping her second finger in her other hand. "Number two—at this point in my life, I can't afford to be distracted from my path. I've been out of school for... what? Almost a year? I'm still here at Swerve, and again, I'm superappreciative," she added for Trevor's benefit, "but this isn't how I imagined my life going. So if I were to meet a guy who I would even consider dating, he would only take up valuable energy that I need to make up for lost time and get back on the track where I should be."

"Sure." Trevor nodded. "And what about number three?" he asked, pouring them each another shot. He would definitely be paying for this in the morning. It had been a while since he'd had this much to drink in such a short span of time.

"Three—" Abby grasped a third finger. "Number three is my favorite. There's nothing a man can regularly give me that my best vibrator can't. And it *won't* leave the toilet seat up." She picked up her glass, sloshing the gold-colored liquor over the sides, spilling over her fingers. *"Sláinte!"* She drank and slammed her glass on the table.

Trevor's eyes widened and he almost choked on the tequila that was still in his mouth. He managed to swallow it without spitting it across the table. "A man can't give you anything more than your best vibrator can?" he laughed. "Is that so?"

Abby winked at him. "Diamonds aren't always a girl's best friend, Trevor. It's a sad truth how replaceable you men are." She shrugged. "Don't look so shattered."

"Honey, I'm not shattered," he assured her, his voice lowered, and he moved in slightly. "I'm just sad. If you think a man is completely replaceable by a battery-operated appliance, then I'm afraid that none of the men you've been with have really, truly rocked your world."

"Rocked my world?"

"That's right," he said casually.

Abby laughed. "Don't worry about my world and how much it gets rocked. Unless you're offering, that is." She raised an eyebrow and reached out and touched his chest. The touch, playful at first, soon turned serious as her fingers lingered.

He had absolutely no response to that. *Was he offering?* So he chuckled instead. That was one of the things he liked about Abby. She was brash, funny and sassy. He liked all of that. She still had her hand on his chest.

Trevor looked down, watching Abby's fingers curl over the material of his shirt, her fingernails singeing the skin underneath. She flattened her palm and smoothed it over his chest, and his breath stilled as he watched her hand move back and forth over his pecs. His muscles tensed in an involuntary reaction. His gaze rose from her fingers to her parted lips. How she made her cherry-red lipstick last all night, he had no idea.

He opened his mouth to speak, but how could he do that when his tongue refused to work in his mouth?

"Abby," he whispered. He barely heard the murmur as it passed his lips, and he didn't imagine that she'd heard it, either. But she looked up at him, her gaze didn't waver, and all that Trevor was aware of was her hand on him, the pounding in his chest and the quick rush of blood that quickly made its way south, away from his brain, depositing directly in his lap.

In the center of his chest, her hand stopped moving, but she kept it where it was, light pressure on his sternum. There was no way that she could have missed the thundering of his heart, threatening to beat clear through his chest. The noise of it in his own ears was deafening. Neither of them spoke, and his eyes pinned on to hers. "Abby," he whispered again.

Their breaths were matched, heavy. And she was so close to him that he could feel her warmth, smell the scent of citrus from her shampoo. She leaned in and looked up at him with large green eyes. A short tendril of hair fell into her eyes, and he reached out and brushed it aside. Need tugged at his chest and his dick. How easy it would be to pull her to him, rip off all of their clothes and make love to her in the booth.

But Trevor took a deep breath. *They were friends*, he maintained. He couldn't have her. As long as she worked for him, he *wouldn't* let himself have her. He was stuck in a volatile situation—the two of them, alone, drinking, and then add to this the fact that he'd seen her naked earlier that evening and knew she was absolutely flawless underneath the clothing that she was wearing…

"We should leave," he murmured, trying to regain a hold on the situation. He placed his hand over hers. At first, he thought he would remove it, but he was powerless to push her away. So he held her there, her palm pressed against his chest.

"Yeah, we should," she said breathlessly. She looked up at him and he peered into her bright green eyes. "Walk me home?"

He nodded. "Yeah."

ABBY BLINKED TWICE. Her brain was telling her that she needed to stand up. That they were leaving. But she couldn't communicate that to her legs. She was frozen in place.

"Abby?" His voice broke through the fog behind her eyes.

"Yeah?"

"Are we leaving?" He removed his hand from hers and she pulled away from him.

"Uh, yeah," she responded. "Let's go." She pushed away from the booth, and Trevor stood, as well. Her cheeks felt hot and his were reddened, too. Her gaze traveled down his front and settled on the impressive bulge behind his zipper, which showed that he was as affected by her as she was by him.

They were silent as they walked to the door. Trevor grabbed their jackets from the backroom and passed Abby hers. When he held the door open for Abby, she stepped outside. The night air had become much chillier since she'd arrived at the club earlier that day, and the small jacket that she had worn over her work clothes had little to no effect in keeping her warm, and, with Trevor weighing on her mind, she hadn't thought to change into the suit she'd worn that day. Thank God she lived only a couple of blocks from the club and their walk would be a short one. Abby wrapped her jacket even tighter and folded her arms over her breasts.

"It sure is cold," she muttered through teeth that almost chattered. "I kind of wish we were back in Vegas."

Trevor's head whipped around to look at her, and Abby knew that his mind had gone where hers had—to their kiss on the roof of Swerve. She hadn't meant to mention it, and she often avoided talking about the city at all, lest they think about what could have been that night, if they hadn't been interrupted, if Abby had let him walk her to her room, if she hadn't seen him talking to another woman when she'd returned to the party. They thankfully hadn't gotten a chance to finish the kiss, but it was obvious that the sexual tension still crackled between them, and at the moment, it was still very close to the surface.

She heard Trevor huff out a breath and he stuffed his hands into his pockets. "Yeah, at least winter is almost over. Spring will be here soon enough."

Abby's bare legs had become numb. And Trevor must have caught her shivering because he moved closer to her and placed his arm around her shoulder, drawing her in, providing her with the warmth she needed.

She could feel the soothing heat emanating from him and she felt herself warm instantly. But the rush of heat didn't just come from Trevor; the flames of arousal were stoked low in her belly and radiated through her. Abby allowed herself to lean into him and closed her eyes from the pleasure. The scent of his spicy cologne did something to her. She inhaled deeply, involuntarily pressing closer into his embrace. She looked up and watched his Adam's apple bob up and down sharply, as he raggedly swallowed. All she would have to do was lift her head a little and she'd be able to place her lips directly on his pulse point. And she might have, too, if they hadn't reached her apartment building.

"Here we are," he announced, removing his arm from her shoulder. She felt the cold air hit her and she immediately mourned the loss of him. He took a deep breath and stepped back. "I'd better go," he said, as if he was trying to convince himself.

They stood on her stoop, and he made no move to leave. She looked up at him, also not eager to end their evening together quite yet. She knew that she couldn't be with him, but, at the same time, she wasn't ready to send him on his way. "Do you want to come upstairs for a bit? We can hang out a little while longer."

Trevor opened his mouth, but it was several beats before he spoke. He nodded, not taking his eyes from her. "Yeah, sure."

She unlocked the front door and they walked to the elevator. The sliding doors closed after them and they rode all the way up in complete silence but for the creaks of the rickety machinery, both Abby and Trevor watching the numbers as the elevator climbed past each floor to the tenth. With a *ding*, the doors separated.

"This way," Abby told him quietly as she left the elevator and turned right. She didn't know what would happen when they got to her apartment. She didn't even know what she wanted to happen. All she knew was that she could feel Trevor walking behind her.

They got to her door and he stood close as she inserted the key into the lock. She walked inside, with him on her tail, and she spun quickly, nearly colliding with the hardness of his chest. And she might have fallen over if he hadn't reached out, one hand encircling her wrist and his other grasping her hip.

It took her a moment to regain her composure. She cleared her throat loudly, and he pulled away. "Would you like another drink? I've got some beer in the fridge, I think."

"Water's fine," he said abruptly, moving away from her. "I don't think I need any more beer."

"Yeah, water." Abby nodded and headed into the kitchen. She needed to get away from him, at least for a moment, to clear her mind without the scent and the pure maleness of him clouding her senses. The cold walk home had sobered her up, but she still couldn't think straight. Abby stood at the sink and, placing both palms on the counter, took a deep breath. She and Trevor had always had fun hanging out, but sometime during the course of the night the air between them had changed. It had become charged. She grasped her wrist where he had held her to steady her. And she could still feel him, as if he were branded onto her skin.

"Pull it together, Abby," she muttered to herself. Why was Trevor able to affect her this way? Why was he able to elicit such a reaction—*desire*—from her, without even trying? Just the feel of his hand on her wrist, his thumb against the point of her rapidly beating pulse, coupled with the intoxicating scent of his cologne, left her with a warm pit of desire low in her belly. Abby reminded herself of her *no-relationships* pact.

But wait!

Like she'd told Trevor, she hadn't given up on sex. She was a grown woman and she could sleep with any man she wanted. It didn't necessarily mean that she had to be in a relationship.

But it wasn't as if Trevor showed anything but a fleeting interest in her. He'd walked her home, but he was just being the good friend she knew he was. And, sure, he'd kissed her, but he'd also put an end once before to a heated moment between them. Abby sighed, and she held a glass under the tap, filling it. She should just see him out and go to bed. Perhaps become reacquainted with the vibrator she'd mentioned earlier.

"Everything okay?" he asked. She hadn't heard him come into the kitchen, and she turned quickly from the shock, sloshing water from the glass all around her.

"I—I'm fine," she stammered. What had happened to her? She could hold her own against a man. She was a modern, liberated, sexual woman. But around Trevor, it seemed that she became a blithering idiot. Her mouth went dry and she drank from the glass she'd filled for him. She took a deep breath. She had to regain control of the situation, but Trevor's presence made it nearly impossible. She drank the rest of the water and put the glass down on the counter.

Trevor laughed, a deep chuckle that rose from his throat and settled around her. "Was that supposed to be mine?" he asked, referring to the now-empty glass.

"Oh, right." Her laugh was shaky. "I knew I was forgetting something." She turned back to the sink to fill his glass.

He came to her and put his hand over hers. "Never mind. It's fine. I don't need water," he said. As they stood in close proximity in her tiny kitchen, she decided right then and there—swearing off relationships or not—she wanted this man.

"Trevor…" she breathed, unable to form the words she wanted to say, the questions she had for him.

"Yeah?" The heat in his low voice echoed that in her own.

"Why didn't we ever hook up?" she asked, unsure of what had happened to the filter between her barely functioning brain and her mouth. "Do you want me?"

His eyes widened. He obviously didn't expect her to ask him that question. "Um…" He exhaled. "Well, I guess we didn't hook up…" He trailed off again, as if searching for a reason, and then shook his head. "Because you were my employee?" His voice rose as if he were asking a question and not making a statement or giving her a reason. "We're friends? The timing was never right?" He paused. "And the fact that I want you more than any other woman just made all of those things that much tougher."

He'd said it. *He wanted her.*

"What about you?" He brought his fingers to her short hair and trailed them through the strands. "Why do think we never hooked up? And, better yet, why did you run away to your room after we kissed in Vegas?"

"I thought you had forgotten that even happened."

The hand in her hair dropped to cup her cheek. "How could I forget something like that? But why did you run away?"

She closed her eyes and leaned into his palm, reveling in the power and the warmth of the hand on her cheek. "I don't know. I was scared, I guess. Maybe the whole giving-up-on-men thing."

Trevor gave a thoughtful nod. "And how's that been working out for you?"

"I've managed to keep all the guys at bay the past couple of months. So, I'd say it's going pretty well."

He kept getting closer. "And what do you think we're doing here right now? If having a relationship is off the table, why am I in your kitchen with my hands on you?"

"I don't know." She steeled herself and straightened. "I'm really liking it, though." She sighed. "But I've been wondering if we can still see each other, *like this*, without having a *relationship*?"

"Like this?" he asked, his smirk telling her that he was teasing her. "You mean in your kitchen. We can be friends in your kitchen, Abby. We don't need to have a dreaded *relationship* to do that."

Abby rolled her eyes. "Be good," she chided. "You know what I mean. Just hear me out."

"Okay, I'm sorry." He laughed. "What do you suggest?"

"You know, it might be amenable to both of us if we consider having one of those, you know, friends-with-benefits type things…" She trailed off.

Trevor said nothing for a while, and she was afraid that he might leave. But a smile played on his lips, and she could tell he was considering it. He reached out to her, his hands gripping her hip. "Friends with benefits?" he asked, moving closer.

"Yeah." She shifted closer to him. "Do I need to spell this out for you? I'm suggesting that we—you and I—we could sleep together, have sex, but not have to endure any of the trappings or the ties of an actual relationship. Because I really don't need that in my life right now." *Or ever, really.*

Trevor narrowed his eyes. And they pierced through

her. He straightened, pulling back slightly. And then he laughed. "Abby, are you drunk? Maybe I should leave and you can just go to bed."

"No, I'm not drunk," Abby protested with a laugh. Her voice softened. "I'm not drunk," she assured him, placing her palm on his chest, reminiscent of the way she had touched him before. She smoothed the fabric on his chest, delighting once again in the firm, tight muscles under his shirt. "This is all pretty nice. But just so you're absolutely certain and don't have to feel bad about any of this, I promise that I'm not drunk." She stopped for a beat before whispering, "I'm just extremely turned on by you. Plus, it's been a *really* long time since I've had sex."

His eyes widened briefly. He cocked his right eyebrow, and he stepped a little closer. "How long?"

Her mind went foggy; she could only smell his cologne and the male scent that emanated from his skin. And she realized that she had no idea what he was asking. "What was that?"

His hand returned to her hip and he drew her in. "How long has it been since you've had sex?" The murmur in his voice sent a vibration through her entire body.

Oh, right, that.

"A little over three months. Not that I've been counting," she confided. Except she had been counting. It had been a long, hard break.

"Three months," he repeated. "That is quite a while," he agreed, his thumb rubbing small circles. Her shirt had ridden up slightly and his thumb was connecting with the bare skin of her waist. His skin on hers made it impossible for her to think straight.

"I can't imagine that you've ever gone that long," she said, looking down at the movement of his thumb.

Trevor stopped his delicious circulations on her waist and stiffened. "What makes you say that?"

She shook her head and ignored his question. She shouldn't have mentioned that. His very active sex life wasn't any of her business. At that moment, she had Trevor in her kitchen, his hands on her body.

She straightened and brought them back to the topic at hand. "So, how about it?"

His thumb charted a path over her bottom lip. He was silent for a beat. "How about what?" he asked. She glanced down and smiled at the impressive way that his pants were tented.

Abby dropped her hand on the firmness of the erection through the material of his pants. She smiled at the hiss he made as he drew a quick breath of air through his teeth. She trailed her fingertips over his remarkable length and smiled, knowing that she held such power over him.

"Trevor—" she squeezed lightly, turned on by the groan that escaped his throat "—do you want to be my friend?" She leaned in and stood on the tips of her toes, pressing her lips to the warm skin below his scruffy jaw. She delighted in the way his five o'clock shadow scraped against her chin. "With benefits?"

All Abby heard and felt was Trevor's groan as it rumbled from his throat. Then he wrapped his fingers around the back of her head and pulled her to him. Their lips met with passionate fury. Not the short, tentative kiss that they'd shared at the rooftop bar in Las Vegas. That kiss had promised more, but they'd been interrupted. This kiss *was* more. Heated. Like water sizzling on a hot pan, the months of sexual tension that had bubbled between them boiled over as they grabbed at each other frantically and kissed against the door of her fridge.

Trevor's hands slid up and down her body, exploring her curves, pushing her clothing out of the way. His lips and tongue traveled over her jaw to her neck, where they reached the sensitive spot inside the hollow of her collarbone. She moaned in satisfaction but then yelped when he nipped her skin between his teeth.

He withdrew his mouth, but he didn't move his body as it pressed against hers, sandwiching her between his hard, warm front and the cold of the fridge door. She faintly heard the magnets clatter on the tile floor. She couldn't do anything about them, however. Not while he was standing next to her, against her. His dark eyes regarded her, his gaze going right through her.

"Christ, Abby," he muttered on a harsh exhalation with a shake of his head. She sobered, suddenly terrified that he would say it was all a mistake and leave her a disheveled, wanting mess in her kitchen. But, instead of leaving, he pushed in again, pressing into her. She could feel the hard length of him against her belly. Thankfully, he kissed her once more, and brought his lips to her ear, and whispered, "Where's your bedroom?"

4

"OFF THE LIVING ROOM," Abby panted, gesturing blindly. "The end of the hallway."

"Perfect," he muttered. He put his hands on either side of Abby's waist and lifted her until her legs wrapped around his waist, locking at his back. She weighed next to nothing in his arms, and, with his hands cupping her perfect backside, he made his way to her bedroom. She was still wearing her shoes and the stiletto heels stabbed sharply into his lower back. But he could barely feel it. He didn't care. The only thing he could focus on was getting her to a bed and ripping her clothes from her body, as quickly as possible. He kissed her as he walked, and he could barely tell where he was going. All he knew was her warm mouth and her hands as they gripped his shoulders and ran through his hair.

When they finally got to her room, he stood in the center of the floor and held on to her. He kissed her once more and then put some distance between them, searching her face for a sign that she was going to change her mind. He found none. And if he couldn't tell if she wanted it to happen just as badly as he did, he was more than certain when she squeezed her thighs around his waist, drawing him in for another kiss. He moaned and walked her to the bed, stopping when his knees hit the edge of her mattress. He slowly lowered her, following her down until he was lying on top of her, not once breaking their kiss.

He leaned back and considered his current position, on his knees between her thighs. He never once believed that he would have the opportunity to lie like this with Abby below him, her hair mussed and her smile wanton, and her hooded eyes looked up at him.

"So, this is happening?" he asked. He held his breath as he waited for her response. If she said no, he would leave and take care of himself before he went to bed… every night for the rest of his life.

"It had better be," she replied and he let out a sigh of relief when her arms encircled his neck and she brought him down to meet her.

Trevor couldn't stop kissing her, her taste like the finest wine or a single malt. He wanted to savour her, but he could feel only the need to take her hard and fast. His tongue stroked hers in time with his hips grinding against her, while his hands traveled over her body. He sat back on his knees and hooked his forefingers into the waistband of her skirt and tugged it down. When he reached her high heels, he gently picked up each foot and plucked off each shoe, throwing them over his shoulder so they clattered to the floor behind him He ran his palms over her long, lean legs, all the way down to her ankles. He worked his way back up her body and his hands found the hem of her shirt, and, with her help, he pulled her shirt over her head, until she was left in just her bra and panties.

He had never before reveled so much in undressing a woman. But with Abby—*with Abby*—it was already different. He wanted to take his time, to discover her. See what made her giggle, moan, cry out in pleasure. She lay on the bed, her perfect form in repose before him. He drank her in. He wanted to touch her, taste her, but first he would have to get rid of the small scraps of satin that stood between him and every inch of her flawless body.

He unhooked the clasp of her bra and pushed the straps aside, over her shoulders, and then her perfect, pert breasts were on full display in front him, and he had all night to take her in.

Trevor heard Abby's sigh when his lips grazed her collarbone and he drew his tongue down and over her chest. "I don't know why we didn't do this before," she whispered.

"Because we're stupid, stupid people." He chuckled before capturing the rosy tip of one of her breasts between his lips. She instantly responded with a moan, arching her back, which thrusted her chest into his face. Trevor feasted on her. While he tongued one sensitive bud, he toyed with the other using his fingers, and then he alternated. He could have stayed there all night, but the way that she ground against his still-denim-clad thigh told him that she needed his attention lower.

She didn't need to plead her case for long. He lowered his head, not content to remain in one place when there was still so much of Abby to explore. He needed to taste all of her. He trailed his tongue down the midline of her trim tummy, dipping lightly to rim her belly button until he found himself, shoulders between her smooth thighs, at the barrier of her satin panties. They were small but he wanted them gone, so he pulled at the edge and she obliged, lifting her hips, bringing her heat closer to his waiting lips.

She was perfect everywhere. His fingers found her warm and wet. She was ready, but he wasn't going to take her just yet. There was still so much he wanted to do. He stroked her and she whimpered and shook slightly under him. She was close. But not before he tasted her.

His mouth descended upon her, feasting hungrily. He barely heard the cry that tore from Abby's lips. His lips and tongue danced about her most sensitive flesh, and she writhed below him. He put his hands on her hips to hold her in place. Before long, he could feel the change in her body and her breathing increased. He knew that she was close and he stayed with her. He looked up at her face, and her mouth was open, soundless, and she began to shake wildly. She called his name, a breathless gasp, and she stiffened beneath him.

He stayed with her as she came back down to earth, gently drawing out her pleasure for as long as he could. He raised his head to look at her, grinning. "Jesus, Abby, you're incredible." His eyes swept over her body. "You're gorgeous."

She sighed with the aftereffects of her orgasm. "And you're still quite dressed," she noted with an arched eyebrow.

"So I am…" Trevor agreed, looking down at himself. He pushed himself up to stand and, without taking his eyes away from her, he unbuttoned his shirt and unsnapped his pants, quickly divesting himself of his clothing.

IT WASN'T THE first time that Abby had seen Trevor shirtless, but in her bedroom, the context of their relationship had completely changed. She was entirely riveted by his broad chest, rippled abdominal muscles, muscled thighs, powerful forearms and the tattoos that ran up his arms. He was still wearing his tight, black boxer briefs. He hooked his thumbs under the waistband of his shorts and she held her breath, waiting for the big reveal.

He started to lower them and she was treated to a peek at the pronounced V of his hips. She brought her lip between her teeth in anticipation. But he stopped abruptly and turned to her. "Do you have a condom?"

"In the bedside table, top drawer," she said, absently gesturing with her hand, not taking her eyes off his body.

He smiled broadly, flashing white teeth. "Good," he said, reaching over into the drawer. Abby laughed when Trevor extracted a handful and tossed them onto the bed beside her, and then he took his spot on top of her. He supported his weight on his forearms and kissed her again.

Abby reached down inside his boxers and wrapped her fingers around his remarkable length, encircling him, stroking him. He moaned into her mouth, but it turned into a gasp when she squeezed him lightly. She giggled.

"If you don't stop that, this isn't going to last long," he warned her, breaking away from her mouth. He took her hand in his and removed it from his shorts. He held both of her wrists in his hands, effectively pinning her to the mattress.

"Well, then, let's get the show on the road," she demanded.

She watched Trevor as he crawled back over her, lowered his boxers and threw them to the side. He grabbed one of the condoms and rolled it over his cock under her unwavering gaze. He primed himself at her entrance and pushed inside. She may have been sated briefly, but it hadn't been enough for her, and she was desperate for him again. She gripped his shoulders and wildly bucked her hips to meet each of his powerful thrusts. She couldn't get enough, but neither could he, it seemed.

They moved together, in perfect sync, until Abby felt her own climax building. She cried out once again, a sharp shriek. Trevor increased the pace of his hips as he thrusted into her. Abby clawed at his shoulders and his tattoo-covered biceps, and she squeezed him. She sighed with sweet relief and he came with his own hoarse shout.

When they'd settled and their breathing had returned to normal, Trevor rolled away to dispose of the condom in the nearby wastebasket. When he returned to the bed, he lay on his back, next to her, their arms touching. Neither of them said anything and the only sound in the room was the leveling of their breaths, in tandem.

"Abby?" he said after several moments, quiet, cautious. "You okay?" Her eyes were closed and she felt him turn to her. He reached out, pushing strands of hair away from her face, lightly tracing her high cheekbone.

She nodded and finally looked at him with a smile. "I am definitely okay." She took a deep breath. "That's something that we have never done together before."

Trevor smiled, and she sighed as his hand whispered over her heated skin. He reached the curve of her hip. He squeezed gently.

"And I can admit that I was wrong," she murmured.

"About what?"

"About thinking that my vibrator could completely replace a man." She sighed. "It certainly can't do that."

5

ABBY YAWNED AND laid her head on her arms on the kitchen countertop, while she not-so-patiently waited for her coffee to finish brewing. She always considered her coffee wait time to be the longest stretch of any morning. She yawned again, watching the delicious black liquid, her lifeblood, drip from the filter into the glass carafe and she relished the aroma. Like every morning, she needed her caffeine fix, but this morning she couldn't even think about keeping her eyes open.

She somehow managed to look up and, her eyes blurry, checked the time on the digital clock on the microwave. 10:35 a.m. It wasn't early, but she and Trevor had stayed up until dawn. Her eyes widened, suddenly more awake when she pictured Trevor above her, underneath her, inside her.

And speaking of... She heard the shower turn off. He must be finished in the washroom. He'd invited her to join him but she politely declined. She'd thought that showering together would breach the wall of non-intimacy that she'd put in place. Yes, it sounded ridiculous, considering that she and Trevor had obviously been intimate the night before. But he'd respected the boundary and he'd showered alone. The coffee was still brewing a couple of minutes later when he walked into the kitchen, wearing last night's clothes, shirt sleeves rolled to his elbows, and a broad smile. His hair wet and slicked back, he picked up his jacket from where he'd dropped it the night before.

"Smells good," he said, nodding to the coffeepot.

"Yeah, it's almost ready. Want some?"

"No." He shook his head. "I've got to get over to the bar. I've got a couple of appointments lined up." He rubbed his eyes. "You know, I'm surprised I'm not more hungover."

"Yeah," Abby agreed. "Me, too. I guess it's a good thing that we sobered up before taking it to the bedroom last night."

"Yeah, about that," he said. "I didn't mean to fall asleep here."

"I know. It was pretty late," she assured him. "It's fine. Don't worry about it."

As Abby walked him to the door, a small niggling of awkwardness made its way to the forefront. "So, I'll see you tonight at the bar," she said. And for the first time, she wondered if she would be able to work with him, now that they'd spent the night together.

He nodded but said nothing. He wouldn't take his eyes off her, and she felt herself drawn back under his gaze.

"Last night was fun," she said.

He laughed and leaned in, kissing her on the cheek. "It really was." He reached out and then grazed her cheek with his fingertips. "I'll see you tonight." He turned down the hallway and headed for the elevator, and Abby couldn't tear herself away to go back into her apartment until he'd rounded the corner. She closed the door and leaned against it. She and Trevor had spent hours together in bed the night before, but when he disappeared around the corner...

Oh, hell, she still wanted him.

"God, show some restraint, Abby," she muttered, as she pulled the carafe from the coffeemaker before it had finished brewing. She poured the coffee into her favorite mug, ignoring the sizzle of the drips hitting the burner plate. She sipped the dark liquid—no cream, no sugar—and sighed with bliss. There was no better way to start a morning.

Well, there was probably *one* better way to start a morning, she considered as she once again imagined the way that Trevor had woken her up—pulling her leg over his and entering her from behind, barely awake, bringing them both to climax with several solid thrusts, as the early morning sun poured in through the window.

The perfect way to start a morning.

As the morning wore on, Abby finished her coffee and did some light housekeeping, things she'd neglected to do since she started working at Swerve. She did everything she could to fill the time until she would go to work and see Trevor again. Not that she *needed* to see Trevor again. She was cleaning the bottom of her refrigerator when she felt her cell phone vibrate on the counter above her. She picked it up and pushed Talk.

"Hello?"

"Abigail Shaw?" the woman on the other end asked.

"Yes."

"Abigail," she continued, "this is Julie from Bon Temps Marketing. You met with us last Wednesday."

Bon Temps? Abby vividly remembered interviewing with them. It was number one on her list of places she wanted to work. She had *really* wanted that job, but because she hadn't heard from them in over a week, she'd figured that she didn't get it. "Yes, of course. But please call me Abby."

"Abby. Very good. I'm calling you today to offer you the account executive position we are looking to fill."

Abby nearly choked on her coffee. She fondly remembered her meeting with Julie. Bon Temps was a young, hip firm, located in an open-concept office with an air hockey table and a small basketball court. They were new, and even though they didn't have the established name and reputation of some of the bigger and older firms in Montreal, she'd felt at home there, and she wanted to be a part of the team that brought the firm the fame and prosperity for which they were destined.

She half listened as Julie outlined the job offer. The description, salary and benefits were better than she could have hoped. When Julie was finished, Abby was silent for a moment, letting the information sink in. It was actually happening.

"Are you still there, Abby?" Julie's voice brought her back to reality. "Are you accepting the job offer?"

"Yes! I'm still here. I'm sorry. But yes, of course, I'd love to accept. Thank you so much," Abby blathered on in excitement. She grimaced. *Stay cool, Abby*, she scolded herself mentally.

"Great!" Julie responded. "We can't wait to start

working with you. Today's Friday, but we were hoping you could start on Monday. Does that sound good?"

"It sounds great. I'll see you then! Thank you so much." Abby ended the call, put the phone on the counter and loudly exhaled. She looked around her apartment and smiled. She was afraid to move, as if she were still in bed, deep within in a dream. This was exactly what she wanted. She was on the cusp of an amazing career and she knew it. She could finally stop working at Swerve.

With Trevor.

A frown turned her lips downward as she thought of him, and a sadness crept up on her. While working at the bar wasn't her career of choice, she loved working with him. And she wondered if they would even see each other anymore if they didn't spend time together behind the bar. She checked the clock and figured that he was probably at the bar, so she picked up her phone and dialed Trevor's number.

He answered on the first ring. "Hey, Abby, what's up?" he asked, his baritone sending a pleased thrill through her system.

She opened her mouth, about to tell him her big news, but she decided it would be better to tell him in person. "Still at the club?"

"Yeah, I'm just taking a quick break. What's up?" he asked again.

Abby ignored his question once more, and she remembered that he probably hadn't stopped to eat before diving into work. "Have you eaten yet?"

"Not yet," he said. "I did put on a pot of coffee, so that's basically breakfast."

"I haven't eaten, either. Listen, I'll be by in about ten minutes, all right? I'll bring doughnuts."

"What's going on, Abby?"

"I'll tell you when I get there. See you soon."

TREVOR SAT IN his office. The smell of the spilled vodka from the day before lingered and, when he looked around, he could still picture Abby standing in the room the day before, almost naked. He could see her flat stomach, adorned with a jewel piercing; her breasts with perfect, upturned nipples that just begged for his hands and his mouth. Had he known at that point that this would be just the beginning of how he'd spend the next twenty-four hours...

Just thinking about her, he felt all of his blood rush to his crotch, his cock thickening against his jeans. How could he be expected to get any work done with Abby coming by soon? *What is she up to anyway?* He didn't care, he just looked forward to seeing her again.

But he had a few things he wanted to do before she got there. He took out the staff schedule, which he needed to finish. While Trevor worked more than sixty hours a week at Swerve, he spent most of that time on his managerial duties and making sure that everything was running smoothly with regard to actual club operations. His time serving was limited, but the shifts he did work—Wednesday through Saturday nights— were the same shifts that Abby worked.

He mused over what her big news could be, why she was coming by when they'd just seen each other. Abby was funny, vivacious and hardworking, and she was the sexiest woman he had ever met. What would he do without her at the bar?

He pushed the schedule away with a sigh, not able to concentrate on it anyway, and picked up a newspaper, flipping through the pages until he opened it to the real estate section. As he did every day, he scanned through the commercial listings until he came across one ad that he'd read many times in the last several months. He picked up a pen and circled it.

The space for sale was a bar—more of a pub, really. Shanahan's had been closed after the death of the original proprietor and put on the market, *at a steal*, by the man's family, who had no interest in continuing operations. He knew exactly what the establishment looked like, its reputation and its history. It was a bar that he'd frequented. One where, a lifetime ago, he'd been employed.

He stared wistfully at the black words of the ad, and he imagined himself back behind that bar. *When it's his own bar.*

Trevor had already saved enough money for the down payment, but he just didn't know if he was ready to take the plunge. He knew almost everything about running a bar but not about *owning* one. But he needed to act soon. The property wouldn't be on the market for much longer. He knew that now was the time for him to buy it.

He was so wrapped up in his daydreams and rereading the words in front of him that he barely heard the door to his office open. He looked up and saw Abby come in holding a tray with two large coffees and a box of doughnuts. He put down the paper and stood, meeting her and relieving her of her load.

"Checking the personal ads?" she asked him with a smirk. "Any single females looking for a roll in the hay with hunky, tattooed, motorcycle-riding bar managers?"

He was quick to grab the paper and stuff it into a desk drawer before she could see the circled ad. "Just reading the sports section," he said, waving it away with a dismissive hand and sitting at his desk.

"Go local sports team!" Abby cracked as she sat in the chair across the desk from him, and Trevor laughed, knowing that she didn't follow sports of any kind, despite the fact the city was home to a National Hockey League franchise.

"So..." Trevor said. He opened the box and retrieved a doughnut that had been dipped in chocolate. He bit into it ravenously. He hadn't realized that he was so hungry. He really needed to stop skipping breakfast. He sipped some coffee to help him swallow the huge chunk of pastry that he'd put in his mouth.

Smooth one, Jones, he scolded himself as he tried to swallow.

"So," he said again once his mouth was clear. "What's this big news that you refused to tell me on the phone?"

Abby flashed a brilliantly wide smile that always managed to hit him low in his stomach. "Well, I just accepted a job offer."

"I knew it! That's great!" Trevor whooped and slapped the desk with his palm. He stood and came around the desk and hugged her. "Congratulations!"

Her arms also wrapped around his waist, and he involuntarily pulled her closer. He heard a muffled "thank you" against his chest. Her warm breath seeped through the material of his shirt, and, as the memory of how he'd held her the night before returned to him,

Trevor was forced to pull away before he wouldn't be able to.

They moved apart, not looking at one another. "When do you start?"

"Monday," she said. "But don't worry, I can still work tonight and tomorrow."

"Thanks. But, you know, you don't really have to. I'm sure I can get one of the guys to cover your shifts if you want the weekend to get ready to start your new job."

She flashed a grateful smile in his direction. "That would be great. I'd really appreciate it. Hopefully, I'll be able to get my sleep schedule back on track. Thanks so much."

"It's no problem." He leaned back in his chair. "So, tell me all about your new job."

She quickly gave him the rundown, and he could see how excited she was to start. He was happy for her, but he sure as hell would miss her, her energy, her infectious spirit.

"I should get going," she announced, standing and plucking two doughnuts from the box. "I've got to pick up some more work clothes. I've got to look nice on Monday morning."

Trevor nodded. She wouldn't need to work very hard to look nice. "Good luck," he said and waved as she practically skipped out the door. Then he sat at his desk, ready to get back to work.

He frowned again. Sure, he was thrilled that Abby had a new job. She was his friend and he only wanted the best for her. But he felt a sharp hollow in his chest. He was really going to miss her. He glanced down at the drawer where he had stuffed the newspaper, took out the paper and smoothed it once again over the real estate section.

If Abby could start a new chapter in her life, so could he. He was going to buy Shanahan's.

As if a lightbulb had turned on over his head, Trevor sat up straight. He was going to do it. He booted up his computer and did an internet search for entrepreneurship and business administration programs happening at nearby colleges. Sure, taking classes would really eat into his free time and the time he spent at Swerve, but he needed to know the *business* side of bar operations—reading financial statements, business law and regulations, and other things that Jamie and the company took care of—before he opened his own bar. If he was going to do it, he was going to do it right.

He looked through the descriptions of various business programs until he found one that fit his needs and would give him the skills and the knowledge to run his own business. He clicked the mouse and opened the online application form for a course that would only take him about six months to complete. The classes were scheduled for early in the morning, so he would be able to attend class, be done by noon and then still have time to take care of his managerial duties at the bar. He took a deep breath and hit Submit.

He read the words on his computer screen. *Thank you for submitting your application.* He smiled and then pulled out his cell phone and dialed the number of the real estate agent listed in the paper.

Trevor was on a roll.

6

ABBY OPENED THE door to her apartment and checked the clock on the wall across her. 10:30 p.m. She had been working at Bon Temps for a little more than a month, and since her first day she had spent many evenings in the office, as had everyone else on the team. It was normally well into the night before she arrived home. She was working crazy hours, but she absolutely loved every minute of it. She had earned several accounts of her own in her short time there, which was another benefit of working for a smaller firm, and she had been building fantastic relationships with all of her coworkers, bosses and clients. It turned out that Bon Temps was a great fit for her own open personality.

Abby went directly to her bedroom, and when she took off her clothes, she opened her already-full hamper. She put her suit in it and frowned when the lid wouldn't fully close. She didn't have any time to devote to doing laundry, and she would have to make a stop at the dry cleaner on her lunch break the next day—if she didn't have to work through it, that is. She saw something black bunched behind the plastic receptacle, and she knelt down to retrieve it. Straightening it out, she saw that it was her Swerve tank top. The thought of Trevor brought a smile to her lips. They'd texted each other a little, but Abby hadn't even seen him since that day in his office when she'd told him that she'd gotten the job. He had been so happy for her. But all that she could recall of that meeting was the way his arms felt wrapped around her. She missed him.

Every night when she went to bed, she relived their night together. The way he'd touched her, kissed her, *rocked her world*... They'd agreed to be *friends with benefits*, but she'd only benefited once from that arrangement. Well, technically, she'd benefited *three times* but it was only one night in total, she reasoned. Maybe it was time to get together again.

It had been way too long since she'd seen Trevor and she hadn't been with another man since. She stood and grabbed her cell phone to send him a quick text.

Hey. Are you busy tomorrow night? Or are you working? It feels like we haven't seen each other in ages. Want to get together?

She had to wait only a couple of seconds before her phone vibrated in her hand.

Sure. What do you have in mind?

Want to go to Charlie's?

She suggested a sports bar just a couple of blocks from Swerve. She noted that it was a Thursday night, and she was curious why he wasn't behind the bar.

You aren't working tonight?

She waited a little longer for a response this time. But his response was simple and perfunctory.

I haven't been working behind the bar much lately. But Charlie's sounds great. See you then.

Abby smiled and threw her phone on the bed. She walked in her underwear into the bathroom to get ready for bed. Nervous excitement crackled in her belly and spread to every other part of her body. She couldn't wait to see Trevor. She missed her friend, but she wondered where the night would take them. Either way, she felt that they had a lot of catching up to do.

CHARLIE'S, A WELL-ESTABLISHED local sports bar, adored by locals, tourists and professional athletes, was one of Trevor's favorite spots. The place was unpretentious, laid-back and completely dedicated to customer service and treating every patron equally, doting similarly on their regulars, notables and newbies. Every person who stepped inside the door was a VIP.

He sat at his regular table and looked around. Another busy night, as was usually the case when there was a Canadiens game on television. The hoots and hollers of the raucous crowd made Trevor smile. These were his people. He belonged in a place like this. He might have run operations at Swerve, but he would not normally patronize a club like that—a place with a dress code, VIP sections and massive lineups. He liked his bars casual, where people from all walks of life could talk and mingle over a beer. His bar would be like that. Casual, fun.

He had just placed his drink order, an IPA from a local brewery that he'd never tried. He took a sip and hummed appreciatively. He would have to look into getting it at his bar, when it opened. When he saw Abby walk in, he smiled and raised his hand. The excited gleam in her eyes and her bright smile as she walked toward him made him warm. It had been around a month since he'd seen her, and she was just as gorgeous and sexy as he remembered. He didn't want to admit to himself that he had impatiently waited all day to see her, but it also seemed as if she were excited to see him, as well.

When she approached the table, he stood and leaned in to give her a quick hug before they sat. It was a warm night, and she was wearing a light jacket over a short dress and tall boots.

"Sorry, I already ordered a beer. I didn't know how long you would be—"

"Oh, don't worry about it." She waved him off, but it was a testament to the fantastic service of the staff that the same server who had brought Trevor's beer was back immediately to take Abby's drink order.

Abby pointed to Trevor's glass. "I'll have one of those."

"It's good," Trevor assured her. "You won't regret it."

"I trust your taste," she said. When the server left, she looked at Trevor. "So, how have you been?"

"I'm good. Things are good." Trevor said, being purposefully vague. He omitted any information about how he'd gone back to school, studying business administration, nor did he tell her about his purchase of a bar, the sale of which had been finalized just a couple of days ago. There was no reason why he couldn't tell Abby, but he just didn't. He was proud of his recent accomplishments, but he didn't want to tell anyone just yet in the event that he failed. So he switched the conversation around to her. "How is the new job?"

"It's great!" Abby exclaimed. When her drink arrived, she took a sip and closed her eyes in satisfaction. "Oh, that is good. Yeah, I love my job. I get to work with all of these different clients, and I have so many accounts already. It's keeping me busy. I literally haven't done anything *but* work for about four weeks." She cast her eyes around the bar, and he could see that excitement back in her eyes. He was relieved that she was doing so well. "It's good to be out of the office, with an actual person, without discussing work."

"All right," he said, relieved that they wouldn't be talking shop the whole night. "No more work talk."

"Deal," she agreed and sipped her beer.

THEY SPENT THE next several hours talking, eating, drinking and laughing in equal parts, and soon, when the mounted televisions all showed post-game talk shows and they were turned off, they realized that they were the sole occupants in the bar, with the exception of the staff.

It was time to leave, but Abby was reluctant to end her night with Trevor. When she'd walked into the restaurant earlier, she'd realized how much she'd missed him in the past four weeks. They hadn't discussed the night they'd spent together, but Abby was relieved that they were able to fall back into their friendship groove.

However, Abby would be the first to admit that the force of seeing him sitting there, waiting for her, hit her like a truck. He looked gorgeous, wearing a dark gray T-shirt, which stretched across his broad chest and shoulders and showed off many of his tattoos, and jeans that were faded in all the right places. She could have jumped him then, and when he hugged her, she could have dragged him off to her place, where they could go for a second round.

Abby looked around the room and smiled sheepishly at the bar staff, who were patiently waiting for Trevor and Abby, their last two patrons to call it a night so they could go home. She had spent enough time in the service industry to know that they had overstayed their welcome in the now-closed restaurant. "Sorry, guys," she said. And she turned to Trevor. "We'd better go."

"Yeah," he agreed. Before she could reach for it, he took her coat from the back of her chair and stood behind her, holding it out for her to shrug into. "Did you drive here?"

She felt his hands smooth over her shoulders, and she shivered. Not from the chill of the air conditioner but from the familiar streak of desire for him she felt in the pit low in her belly, which warmed her body. "No, I walked." She pulled away from his touch. "We're not far from my apartment. I'll just walk back. It's not a big deal."

"Well, let me walk you home. It's pretty late for you to be out alone."

Abby sighed. She hated the idea that because she was a woman of diminutive stature, she was vulnerable walking alone. She would normally have said no and insist that she's fine on her own, but she wanted to spend every second with Trevor that she could. "All right," Abby said with a smile, walking to the door. "Let's go."

The walk was short, and unlike the first time he'd walked her home, the temperature was warm. Abby fondly remembered when he'd put his arm around her that time and drew her close to keep her warm. His extra warmth had kept her from succumbing to the cold that night, but tonight it wasn't necessary, especially since she could feel his gaze singeing her skin. When they reached her building, she turned to him. "Want to come in?"

He nodded. "Yeah, sure."

She turned on her heel and took his hand, leading him into the lobby and then up to her apartment. When they were inside her place, they sat in the living room, Abby on the couch and Trevor in the nearby chair. Purposefully keeping their distance from each other?

"I had a really good time tonight." Abby spoke first, breaking the silence. "I missed you."

Trevor smiled at her. "I missed you, too."

Abby said nothing for a moment, unsure how to broach the topic of the arrangement they'd talked about a month ago. "Do you remember I suggested we try a friends-with-benefits relationship?"

His eyes snapped up to her face. "Vividly."

"Well—" she took a breath "—why didn't we keep that going?"

Trevor laughed. "I don't know." He shrugged. "We haven't even seen each other and it seems like we've both been pretty busy." He paused. "Would you like to keep it going?"

"Would you?"

"I asked you first."

Abby looked at the floor. Did she want to keep seeing Trevor, without having to worry about it being a *relationship*? She would love nothing more than for him to pick her up from her couch and bring her to her bedroom. She looked up at him and nodded.

Trevor joined her on the couch and took her hand in hers. "Me, too."

Abby smiled, his warmth traveling through her body, along with the pleasant tingle from his closeness. This was going to happen again, and she couldn't wait.

"So, shall we?" he asked with another smile that made her stomach flutter. He shifted to face her.

Yes! "Wait," she said, "it can't be that easy."

"Why not? We're good together. We both want it."

"What if we set some ground rules?"

"Rules? You might be overthinking this, Abby."

Was she overthinking it? *Probably.* "I just need to stop this from getting too complicated." Abby didn't want to risk losing him as a friend. They had gone a month without seeing each other, and she didn't want that to happen again. She couldn't bear it if she lost his friendship.

"Okay, what do you have in mind?"

"Well, remember that I swore off men a couple of months ago?"

"I remember that conversation."

"That's still very much in effect. I'm not looking for a relationship. So, if we do this—" she waved a hand between them "—we have to be careful to keep it purely physical and not to step into relationship territory. Okay?"

Trevor shrugged and leaned back into the couch. "Fine by me."

"So, no dates," she said and looked to him for confirmation.

He nodded in agreement. "No dates. How about no sleepovers?" he suggested "No staying the night."

"Good one."

He went on. "And we should agree that if either of us meets someone, then we end it cleanly. And we stay friends."

"You're good at making rules," she told him.

"Anything else?"

Abby was silent for a moment. She had one. One she'd used in the past. She turned to Trevor, and she looked into his dark eyes. "Don't fall in love."

"I think I can manage that," Trevor told her.

He stood from his place on the chair and went to her. Abby remained seated, and Trevor reached down and cupped her cheek, his fingertips grazing her jaw.

Her eyes briefly fluttered shut at his touch, and his lips took hers in a soft kiss. His tongue swept across her lips and she parted them, opening to him. His tongue stroked her, and she felt herself succumb to the pleasure that she knew he would offer.

She squealed with surprise when he lifted her from the couch and effortlessly threw her over his shoulder.

"What are you doing?" she asked him, with a laugh. "Put me down."

"I don't think so," he said. And he slapped her sharply with a strong, open palm on her backside.

His strong arms held her in place while she squirmed over his shoulder. Trevor walked her to the bedroom. When they got there, he threw open the door and gently, but with wild flourish, dropped her onto the bed. She laughed heartily, as he joined her in the center of the mattress, swinging one of his legs over her, straddling her hips.

He leaned over her, supporting his weight on his forearms and he kissed her again. This wasn't the sweet, gentle caress of his lips that she'd felt moments before. This time, his kiss was rough, demanding and consuming. She threw her head back against her pillow and he took the opportunity to kiss her neck. His teeth scraped her sensitive skin, and his tongue traced the delicate line where her neck met her shoulder.

"Fuck, Abby," he muttered into the crook of her neck, his breath washed over her, and she moaned in response, and lifted her hips, desperate to feel a release from the pressure that was already starting to build deep in her core.

"God," she sighed. "I've wanted this again since the last time we were together."

"Me, too, babe," he growled, before his mouth again captured hers. He hiked her dress up over her hips and quickly pulled down her panties. His movements were so quick she could barely keep up with him.

With his large hands, Trevor gripped her hips and turned her, making her gasp. Before Abby even realized what was happening, she was lying on her stomach.

"Trevor." Her voice was barely a whisper, as he pulled her hips up to meet him. He was still wearing his jeans, but she couldn't have missed the hard steel of him behind the denim.

She might have still been wearing her dress but her bottom half was still completely exposed to him. He cupped her, and then dragged his fingers through her hot, wet folds. The touch sent shockwaves throughout her body, and she shuddered.

"Mmm, Abby," he hummed. "You're so wet."

Her face was in her pillow and she turned her head, resting on her cheek, so she could breathe. "Trevor, now," she pleaded. She wanted him. She needed to feel him. She was ready.

He slid a finger inside her, and followed it with another. His fingers curled inside her and he hit her in just the right place. She cried out, and when he used his other hand to slide against her clit, she thought that she might die from the sensory overload. Abby whimpered when he pulled away and smacked her on the ass, hard. The sound of it filled the room, and she cried out again, as warmth spread throughout her. "Now," she demanded.

Abby couldn't see him, but she heard his lusty chuckle, and out of the corner of her eyes, she saw him reach for the bedside table where she kept her condoms, and she smiled, knowing that relief would soon come.

She heard his zipper lower slowly, and the rustle of his jeans as he lowered them. A couple of seconds later, the tip of his cock teased her opening, threatening to enter her, but holding back, playing with her.

With an impatient whine, she arched her back and pushed against him, desperate to feel him inside her.

Trevor laughed again and smoothed his hands over her ass, and after another quick, sharp slap of his palm, he pushed inside.

She screamed in response to him, as he pumped his hips against her backside. His pace was fast, his strokes sure, but he was unrelenting. It was only a minute before she felt a tremble in her core and the pleasure radiated throughout her limbs. Her orgasm hit her with such a force that it threatened to collapse the bed with her tremors. She opened her mouth, but no sound came out, and her arms and legs turned to jelly, sapped of all their strength. She found it difficult to hold herself upright.

Trevor leaned over her and wrapped his arms around her waist, pulling her upright, so that she was kneeling before him as he repeatedly pumped his hips, chasing his own release. Eventually he stilled, and he tightened his grip on her, as he finished, spasming, emptying himself in the condom.

When he pulled his arms from her, releasing her from his hold, she moved away, and she fell to the bed, too exhausted to move, or even fully remove her dress while he disposed of the condom.

When Trevor returned to the bed, his smile was smug and satisfied. Abby could see on his face that he was pleased with himself. And he had every reason to be. He was incredible in bed. She extended her fist to him as he lay down next to her. Trevor bumped it with his own.

Abby looked over at him as she regained her breath and he did the same. They could do it. They could have fun in the bedroom and still remain friends. She was certain of it.

7

THE NEXT MORNING, Trevor yawned as the professor drew class to a close. He found his financial analysis class challenging enough, but that morning he had caught himself about to doze off several times. He wasn't certain if it was a result of the subject matter, the teacher's monotone voice, the high temperature of the room or his exhaustion because of the night he'd spent with Abby.

It had been after five o'clock that morning when he'd left Abby's and made it back to his own apartment, and then he really only had enough time to shower and eat a quick breakfast before the start of his 8:00 a.m. class.

He felt a thrill of excitement, which energized him, when he thought about the hours he'd spent with Abby. He hadn't thought he would ever get the chance to be with her again.

When he closed his eyes, he didn't see the financial formulas or any of the definitions that the instructor was trying to drum into the brains of his students; all Trevor could see was her. Her naked body under him, on top of him, flashes of his hands skimming over her soft skin, the top of her blond head when her lips wrapped around him… He might be tired, but it was well worth it.

Finally, the class was over and Trevor stood to gather his things. He was about to leave the room when he felt a hand on his arm, holding him back. Turning, he saw the young woman who sat behind him every day. The cute brunette with whom he'd exchanged smiles, but no words, before taking his seat every morning.

"Hi," he said. He waited for her to speak, even though all he wanted to do was get home and get a little sleep before he headed to the club.

"Hi there." She smiled broadly. She seemed perky, bubbly. "I'm sorry to bother you. It looks like you're on your way out and everything, but I was wondering, with the midterm coming up and all the assignments, if you had a study group? I mean, it looks like you've got a pretty good handle on what's going on here every day, but I'm having a bit of trouble and I don't really know anyone in class. I didn't know if maybe you wanted to get together sometime and go over some practice questions."

Trevor nodded. A study group was a good idea. It couldn't hurt and he really couldn't afford to fail or do poorly in the course. "Yeah, sure," he agreed. "I'm free Wednesday evening. How does that sound to you?"

"That sounds awesome." She juggled her books and her purse to her left arm and extended her hand to him. "I'm Robin."

Trevor shook her hand. "Trevor. Nice to officially meet you." He bit back a yawn. This schooling and working, not to mention being up all night with Abby, was really catching up to him. Even though he knew that Robin would rather stick around to chat, he had to get home.

"I'm sorry, but I've got to go," he said as he moved to leave.

"Oh, of course," she responded. Her smile never faltered. She was a chipper one. "Oh, wait, take my cell phone number. Text me, and we can set up a time to study for the midterm." She wrote her name and number in her notebook, tore off the paper and gave it to him.

"Thanks, Robin," he said, putting the paper in his pocket. "I'll text you later."

She winked as she walked past him. "I'm looking forward to it." He watched her walk away, hips swaying. In the past, he would have stayed to talk to her. He would have been drawn in by how her jeans molded to her shapely backside or how she flipped her long, wavy hair.

But Trevor barely noticed any of that. Robin was an attractive woman, but he just wasn't interested. All he could think about was the petite blonde with whom he had spent the previous night.

ACROSS TOWN, ABBY sat at the round conference table and tried to focus on the words being said by her colleagues. She guzzled back her coffee, forever thankful for the coffee shop next to her office building and those sent-from-God baristas who helped her with her daily triple-espresso fix. But today they had giggled when she said that she needed an extra shot, an extra boost just to get through the morning.

Abby watched her boss, François, speak, but she could barely hear his words over the vivid images of

Trevor that paraded through her brain. She shook her head, trying her damnedest to wake up and pay attention to the morning meeting.

"With the Ashbourne account, that brings us up to a total of fifteen new clients this month," François announced.

The group cheered loudly, applauding their success.

François held up a hand, attempting to silence them so he could carry on. "So, let's continue, shall we? We can celebrate later," he said with a broad smile. He pushed a button on his laptop and a large projector screen descended from the ceiling, and his presentation started.

"Ashbourne Cosmetics is a local brand. They are one of the top sellers of luxury organic anti-aging solutions and they have expressed an interest in getting back to basics. They're rebranding. They want something new, something fresh. And they want to utilize a Montreal-based marketing company. One that's just starting to get off the ground. And they want us to be that firm." The people around the table buzzed in excitement about the new client. But François continued. "And I would like Abby to take the lead on this."

Upon hearing her name, Abby looked up at her boss and the smiling faces of her supportive colleagues sitting around the table. "Excuse me. What?"

"I want you to be in charge of the Ashbourne account. You're familiar with their products, right?"

"Yes! Of course I am. I'd be honored to head this up." She was absolutely gobsmacked. "Thank you so much for the opportunity," she stammered. "I won't let you down."

"I know you won't." François beamed at her and

passed her a file, which included all of the company's information that she would need to review before meeting with its representatives. He stood. "That's everything for today, guys." The group started to rise. "But first, I want to say thank you to each and every one of you. Without you guys, this business would be nothing. Together, we will make Bon Temps the premier marketing firm in the city and, soon, in the country."

Abby felt a surge of pride. Pride in the work she was doing and in the company that she was a valuable member of. Along with the rest of her colleagues, she applauded, still elated that she had been assigned a huge account but also nervous that she might somehow screw it up. She was so glad that she had gone to work with Bon Temps. She was on a career trajectory she would have never experienced at a bigger firm. This would be her opportunity to prove herself, to show them all that the new girl had the skills to go far in the industry.

If she wasn't so goddamn tired.

Abby walked over to her desk, situated in a corner near the Ping-Pong table. There were no private offices at Bon Temps. It was a completely open office space to "facilitate the flow of ideas and teamwork," as it had been explained to her. She drained the remaining espresso from her cup and then she frowned. She might have to get more caffeine in her system before she started work on the Ashbourne account.

Trevor had absolutely worn her out the night before, and she hadn't slept after he'd left her place early that morning. How could she when her entire body tingled at the memories of how he touched her and kissed her and said all those dirty things to her? Not to forget the anticipation that built within her, the desire to do it all over again? She would sacrifice nights of sleep, days of productivity just to be with him again.

"Hey, Abby." Sarah, another new account executive, came up to her desk. She was smiling. "Congratulations on the big account! I'm so happy for you!"

"Thanks," Abby responded. "It's definitely a surprise."

"You must have a ton of work to do, but I just wanted to let you know that some of us girls are going out for a few drinks after work, and I was wondering if you wanted to join us. We can celebrate you getting Ashbourne while we're there."

Abby smiled. She should get out more. "Yeah, that sounds great."

She was tired. But with Maya gone, she really missed having a girlfriend in the city. Maybe her coworkers could fill the void left by her best friend. Either way, it would be a good way to let off some steam. But first, she had to get to work.

She opened the file folder and began reading the information about Ashbourne. The words and numbers on the paper crisscrossed in front of her eyes. She stood from her desk and picked up her purse to head back to the café next door for another fix.

8

THAT NIGHT, ABBY walked into Swerve for the first time since she'd finished working there. The memories flooded back to her—laughing and joking with her coworkers, hanging out with Trevor. She recalled the night she'd gone there with Maya, when Abby had dared her friend to kiss a sexy stranger. They didn't know that that man would be Jamie, the man Maya was currently set to marry. She walked past the booth where she had reached out and put her hand on Trevor's hard chest.

"Abby, I'm so glad you could make it!" Sarah jumped from the table where she sat with two other women from their firm.

"Thanks for the invite. It's good to get away from the desk sometimes, right?"

Sarah poured Abby a margarita from the pitcher that they'd ordered and handed her the glass. "Here you go. Drink up!"

"Thank you." She took a sip. Not bad, but not great either. Abby took a glimpse at the bar to see if she could tell who made the drinks. Trevor wasn't working, but she didn't have to look to know he wasn't there. She could tell by the subpar taste of the drink. Trevor made a mean margarita. Instead, there were two people she didn't recognize behind the bar. Things were changing all over, it seemed. She shrugged and drank the rest anyway. *Don't look gift tequila horse in the mouth, Abby.*

She sat back and relaxed. After working at the firm for so long, she was happy to be finally really getting to know some of her colleagues. They all seemed like nice women. And when the waitress noticed that their pitcher was empty, they ordered another, and then another, and pretty soon, the DJ starting spinning and the women decided that they wanted to dance.

Abby loved dancing and she must have stayed on the dance floor for hours. But by the early hours of the morning, their group had dwindled, as each of the women decided to go home. Soon, just Abby remained.

Figuring it time to go home, Abby stopped dancing and made her way to the table where her group had been sitting. Obviously, in the busy club, it had already been claimed by another group. Not a big deal, but she remembered that she had had a purse when she came in. But now her purse, which contained her wallet and her keys, was nowhere to be found. *Dammit!* Thankfully she had her cell phone in the back pocket of her jeans.

Her temperature rose and she felt the room start to spin a little. She had to place her hand on a table to steady herself. She shut her eyes. She'd had too much to drink and it was just starting to sneak up on her. But she had the sense to know that she wasn't in a good situation.

She had no idea how she was going to get home. She was impaired, her friends were gone, she didn't think she could walk, couldn't pay for a cab and she didn't recognize any of the staff to ask them for help. So Abby did the only thing she could think of.

TREVOR HEARD THE ringing through the haze of sleep. He opened his eyes, realized it was his cell phone and bolted straight up in bed. His heart rate accelerated as he imagined the worst because why else would someone call him in the middle of the night? He reached for his phone and looked at the screen. Abby.

"Hello?" He could hear the thundering of his heart as he worried that something might be wrong with her.

"Hey, Trev," she said. He could hear music in the background.

"Hey, Abby. Are you okay?"

"Yeah, I'm perfectly fine."

He sighed with relief but furrowed his brow in confusion. Her words were slurred and she sounded drunk. "So, what's up?"

"What do you mean?"

"Why are you calling me at—" he checked the clock on his phone "—2:47 a.m.? Is this a booty call?" he asked her, joking.

"Oh," she said, laughing. He could still hear the driving beat of the music in the background. "I was out with some girls from the office. But now they're gone…and I can't find my purse."

"Are you okay?"

"I'm fine. I'm just a little drunk. But…" she trailed off and blew out a breath "…I was just wondering if you could pick me up?"

He didn't hesitate. He launched himself out of bed

and located the jeans he'd discarded on the floor. "Yeah, of course. Where are you?"

"I'm at Swerve. And it's really weird—I don't recognize anyone here."

Trevor knew what she meant. They had just gone through a major turnover, and he had hired a whole new slate of people. Bouncers, bartenders and cocktail servers were all being trained. "I'll be right there. Don't go anywhere, okay? I'm coming for you."

TREVOR WAS OUTSIDE the club in under ten minutes. He saw Abby immediately, leaning against the outside of the building, her arms folded over her chest. She was wearing a pair of skinny jeans and a tank top—she'd obviously skipped the jacket.

But more disturbing than that was the way she stumbled against the wall at the same time as he saw two men approach her and start talking to her. Trevor quickly parked his car and, without even turning off the engine, jumped out and was by her side. The men looked at her with interest, but Trevor quickly interjected himself between them and Abby.

"Can I help you here, fellas?" He stared them down.

"We're just talking to the lady," one of them replied.

"Well, now I'm talking to the lady," he practically growled. "Get the fuck out of here."

The two men slunk back to the entrance of the club. But before they could enter, Trevor signaled the bouncer to not let them in. Once they were denied entry, they left without any more trouble.

"Hey, Trevor," Abby whispered, tipping her head against the outside wall of the club so she could look up.

"Hey, Abby." Trevor put his arm around her shoulders. She was ice-cold. "You're freezing. Where is your jacket?"

"I left it at the office, Dad," she said, giggling.

Trevor cursed and bundled her into his waiting car. "You're lucky you didn't become hypothermic. Why didn't you wait inside?" He buckled Abby in without any help as her eyes closed and her posture went limp.

It wasn't long before Abby's breathing steadied. He glanced over at her and smiled when he saw that she was asleep. He pulled out onto the road to drive her home. But he remembered that she didn't have her purse, which undoubtedly meant that her keys were probably MIA, as well, so he turned around and drove to his own apartment, instead. At least he could let her sleep before they figured out where her things were.

When he pulled into his parking space, he turned off the engine and touched her shoulder. "Hey, Abby, we're here."

She barely stirred and kept her eyes closed. "Where are we?"

"My place. It's just for the night. Is that okay?"

"Yeah, of course," she muttered, settling back into the seat, as if she was going to continue sleeping there.

Trevor sighed. Thank God he didn't have class the next morning. He was likely going to be up all night with Abby—and not in the way he would have preferred. He walked around to her side of the car, opened the door, unfastened the seat belt and then scooped her up in his arms. There was no way she would be able to make it up the exterior stairs on her own.

The bracing cold stirred her and she wrapped her arms around his neck. "Was I asleep?"

"Yeah." He came up to his door and, balancing

her in one arm, pulled his key from his jacket pocket. When he got inside, he laid her gently on the couch.

"It's so weird. I normally can't fall asleep around anyone."

Trevor wasn't sure why, but he warmed at the thought of Abby trusting him enough to fall asleep. But he quickly passed it off. "Well, it might have something to do with the alcohol consumption," he remarked. "I've never seen you this drunk. How much did you have?"

Abby's eyebrows drew together. "Oh, I don't know. Three drinks? Seventeen? Who's to say?" She laughed. "Although whoever is working tonight, really needs to up his margarita game. They *definitely* weren't as good as yours."

Trevor frowned as he tried to remember who was scheduled. He certainly didn't like that subpar drinks were being passed out to customers. It was an issue he would have to address when he worked again. He didn't want quality of the product to suffer just because he wasn't physically working at Swerve. He felt guilty over it. But, as he looked at Abby, he realized that Swerve didn't matter at the moment. He needed to make sure she was okay.

"So, it was the tequila?"

"No, tequila doesn't normally affect me so much. I think it was the vodka shots that Sarah got for us. I mixed liquor and then I had beer."

"Rookie mistake, Abby."

"I know. *Bad, bad Abby*," she muttered, curling into a ball on the couch.

"Can I get you anything? Some water? Food?"

"I'll take some water. And some toast?" She looked up at him hopefully.

He smiled. "You got it," he said, going in to the kitchen. He lightly toasted a slice of bread for her and poured her a glass of water. When he returned, he sat next to her on the couch.

"Thanks for picking me up." She smiled at him gratefully, accepting the food. "You're a good friend, and I really appreciate it. It definitely could have been trouble."

"It was no problem."

"I'm glad that we can still be friends. I miss having Maya around." She frowned. "That's why I went out tonight. I was hoping to get closer to the girls from work."

"But they ended up leaving you there," he reminded her.

She shrugged her shoulders. "Yeah, I can't put all of the blame on them, though. It was kind of sucky, but I probably should have left when Sarah did. And I definitely should not have had so much to drink. Either way, you were there for me." She leaned on his shoulder. "Thanks. It really means a lot."

"You're just being sappy because you're all liquored up," he joked. But he would admit that he also missed having Jamie around. He shifted and put his arm around her shoulders as she nibbled on her slice of toast. She curled into his side, and her warmth seeped through his clothes to his skin. He tried to stop the small sigh of pleasure that escaped his lips. There was nothing sexual about the contact. But there was something else. Comfort. And he realized just how much he liked it.

"I'm sleepy," she muttered into his T-shirt.

"Well, go to sleep."

"I'm not supposed to stay the night," she told him. "The rules."

Ah, yes. The rules. "Well, why don't we just forget the rules? Just for tonight." He pulled her closer and looked down at the top of her head as she slept. Something bad could have happened to her tonight and he was grateful that she'd called him. He wanted to protect her, and he felt a surge of affection for her overtake him. And, for the first time, he thought that it might be a little tougher to remember the rules than he thought.

9

TREVOR TURNED OFF THE TV. There was absolutely nothing on. He looked at his watch. Six thirty. And he wondered what he even did before he spent almost every night at the bar. And while he knew that he was on the track to bettering himself, he actually missed it. He'd left there over an hour ago, finishing up his work. His staff was confused when he left, as they had expected him to stay and work behind the bar for the night, as he would normally have done.

But things had changed. He'd changed.

He glanced briefly at the textbooks piled on the table. Supposing he would do some studying, he opened one of the books, but he couldn't concentrate on any of the words. Even though he enjoyed the course work, he had excess energy to work off and he was fidgety. Without bartending in his life, a nervous agitation wore on him. He tried reading from the chapter to prepare for his class the next day, but his left leg shook restlessly and his fingers drummed absently on the table. He sighed, slammed the book closed and sat back.

He looked at his phone, sitting on the table. And

before he could talk himself out of it, he dialed Abby's number. Just picturing her made his dick hard. He'd had sex with her just a few nights before. But it wasn't just about the sex. It was great, but he liked being around her. He wanted to see his friend, and maybe she would help him work off the nervous energy he felt.

"Hello?" Her breathy voice on the other end made him smile.

"Hey, do you have any plans for tonight?"

"Not one," she said. "Why?"

"Want to come over?" *Idiot.* He didn't want to appear too needy. "You know, we could watch a movie or something." He tried to play it cool. *Do friends with benefits hang out and watch movies?* That wasn't exactly laid out in the rules. He slapped himself on the forehead.

She laughed. It was a sound that fluttered through him, bringing him pleasure. "Are you asking me to come over to watch Netflix and chill?"

"Yeah, I guess so," he replied. "I just really want to see you tonight." He hated that he sounded desperate and how much he actually needed her. With women, he was used to being in control. Being pursued, not the pursuer.

She paused for a few too many seconds, and he held his breath, thinking he might pass out before she responded. "Want me to bring anything?"

"Just get over here."

"Okay," she finally answered. "I'll be there soon."

ABBY PARKED HER car outside Trevor's apartment building. She smiled. Of course she was smiling. Despite the hangover she'd felt a few days ago when she woke up alone in Trevor's bed—he'd taken the couch—she'd had a fantastic day at work. Work on the Ashbourne account was progressing and she couldn't wait to show them the ideas she'd come up with so far. But that wasn't it. She felt a tremor of energy travel through her body as she looked at the exterior of his building. She was excited to see him and glad he called her. *But that doesn't mean anything. It's not a date*, she told herself. She was excited about seeing Trevor for three reasons. She checked them off mentally: He was a fun guy to hang out with; he was her friend, a good one as he'd proven a couple of nights earlier; and she knew that she was about to be on the receiving end of some stellar orgasms. And she remembered his voice on the phone. *"Just get over here,"* he'd commanded her.

Bossy.

She shuddered. She was a fiercely independent woman, but she wasn't afraid to say she liked that he had called the shots when they were together. He'd told her where he wanted her, what he wanted her to do, while doing what he wanted to do. He was an attentive lover, though. Taking what he sought but all the time conscious of her needs and what she wanted from him.

She felt the shiver of anticipation and desire as she walked up the stairs, drawing closer to his door. She knocked, three sharp raps on the door, and waited what couldn't have been more than ten seconds before he opened the door. And after he did, he quickly pulled her inside and wrapped his arms around her waist, drawing her to him, kissing her.

"Whoa, whoa." She reluctantly stepped back from his embrace, not wanting to want it so much. Her reaction to him scared her and threatened their whole *no-relationship* rule. "What was that?"

Trevor shrugged. "Just saying hello."

She was momentarily apprehensive, but she couldn't help herself. She looked at him, so devastatingly sexy, and then she focused on his mouth, his wicked lips turned up in a devilish grin, and the only thing she could do was kiss him back.

As his lips pressed against hers, he opened his mouth and his tongue swiped against hers. She instantly forgot about the need she felt to reestablish the ground rules of their agreement. This wasn't a relationship. He wasn't allowed to kiss her hello like that whenever she came over. It was just sex, after which she wanted them to remain friends. But, as she twined her arms around his neck, she ignored the nagging voice of reason in her brain. Her hormones, not her brain, were in control as she pushed against him and kneaded the muscles of his shoulders and then his biceps and chest. She was already obsessed with his body.

All day, she had pictured his firm and tattooed body every time she closed her eyes. She had all of the arguments why they couldn't continue on like this sitting at the tip of her tongue, but all she could do was sigh in surrender and collapse against his chest, forgetting every reason as he lowered his head, bringing his warm, demanding mouth to the sensitive spot nestled between her neck and shoulder.

Abby would have to remind him, and herself, of the rules later. *When we're not so distracted.* But right now she let him tug her lightly in the direction of his bedroom.

THEY MADE IT as far as his couch.

The second they reached the living room, Trevor decided that he couldn't wait and pulled her down on the dark brown leather, so that she was lying on top of him, her lean thighs straddling his hips and her mouth fused to his.

With a firm grip on her hips, he held her closer to him, pushing his already-stiff cock against her, feeling her heat through the denim of his jeans and her thin panties. She moaned into his mouth, and his control snapped. He quickly rolled over, pinning Abby to the couch, still at his place between her thighs, nestled in her sweet heat. He kissed her; he couldn't get enough. His hands on her face, her neck, her shoulders, her legs. He was desperate to touch her everywhere.

His hand landed high on the smooth skin of her thigh. He brought his fingers higher and soon they were under her skirt, cupping her and rubbing her through the satin of her panties. He slipped the silky obstruction to the side, finding her wet and warm. He pushed a finger inside her and she gasped, pulling her mouth away from his. He felt her clench against his digit and he added another while the heel of his hand rubbed against her clit. It wasn't long before she started to shake and thrash below him and he knew that she was close.

Trevor was a goner.

Dropping all semblance of decorum or civility, using his free hand, he ripped at her white blouse, tearing the buttons and the material away from her breasts, revealing the champagne-colored bra she wore underneath her shirt. She looked up at him with eyes holding a mix of shock and desire, revealing that she was dangerously close to the edge. He continued his diligent work under her skirt as he roughly pulled down her bra, exposing her breasts. He lowered his head and brought his lips to the rosy bud of one nipple. The second his mouth closed over her, she screamed, her fingernails driving sharply into his shoulders, but he ignored the bite of pain and kissed his way back up to her mouth and took her lips again. His mouth covered hers and he swallowed each of her cries as she shuddered beneath him.

Before her tremors quelled, Trevor moved away and dropped to his knees on the floor in front of the couch. He grabbed the backs of her knees, pulling her to meet him, and slung her legs over his shoulders. Then he brought his lips to her.

"Again?" she whispered, clearly not yet recovered from her last orgasm.

"I need to taste you," he murmured, placing his lips to Abby's sweet center. He kissed her, his tongue swiping long strokes over her sensitive flesh. She writhed under him and he gripped her tightly. He skirted over the tight bud and she shuddered again. With his tongue, he lavished her again and again until she shook and cried out. It took less than a minute for her to come again, but he stayed with her until her quakes subsided. He kissed her, gently, until she sighed. He watched her. Her body was limp, and her eyes were heavy, sated, satisfied. She leaned against the back of the couch, her eyes fluttering shut.

He stood and then took his place beside her on the couch and, in an attempt to sit casually next to her, he pressed his palm against the most painful erection he'd ever had in his life. He looked at Abby and wondered if she had fallen asleep. Her eyes were closed and her breaths steady, and he chuckled as he pulled a throw off the back of the couch and covered her with it.

One of her eyes opened. Perhaps she wasn't in the deep sleep he had assumed she was. "What about you?" she raised her eyebrow, glancing into his lap at his obviously tented jeans.

Trevor shrugged. "The night is young and I can wait until later. It's not a big deal if you're tired and want to rest." And he definitely didn't want to make her feel like she had to reciprocate in any way.

She pursed her lips and shook her head. "I don't think so," she said. "That isn't how I roll. I don't leave my *friends* hanging…or standing like that." She dropped a hand to his crotch and rubbed him appreciatively through his jeans. He moaned and she pushed the blanket from her and moved over him, straddling him as he sat on the couch. He smiled before she kissed him. Trevor should have known that Abby wouldn't leave him wanting.

She gripped his shoulders and, again, her nails dug painfully into his skin. He didn't care. She kissed him hard, her tongue twining with his own. He could still smell her sex on his mouth, and dammit if his dick didn't nearly tear right through his zipper. He ran his hands up and down, over her body and her firm backside. She ground herself into him and moaned, the vibration in his mouth increasing his need. It had to be now. He held her in place, hands on her hips and flexed his hips upward to press his stiffened cock against her now-sensitive flesh. She broke away from his mouth and squealed. His lips found her neck and kissed down her chest, to her breasts that were still exposed, propped up with the foam of the cups of her bra. He suckled her once again, using his lips, teeth and tongue to make her cry out.

They were both still mostly dressed, and she pulled away from him, out of range of his mouth. He reached for her, but her fingers started tackling his shirt, unfastening his buttons, kissing her way down his heated flesh. He moaned and threw back his head, shutting his eyes. She pushed open his shirt and smoothed her palms over his pecs and down his stomach. Her fingers simultaneously tickled and then scorched his skin, and he was certain that if he opened his eyes and looked down, there would be little trails of fire blazing from her manicured nails. Nothing felt better than her hands and mouth on him, and as she teased him, slowly working her way over him, he was caught between wishing she would go lower and wishing it would never end. The feel of her, her scent, her taste still on his lips, the delighted noises she made as she explored his body— it all combined to bring him so near the edge, even though his cock hadn't even yet entered the equation.

Trevor had never been trigger-happy. But with Abby touching him, he was close to embarrassing himself like a teenager during his first time with a girl. There had been so many unbelievably sexy women in his past, and he was always in complete control in bed. But Abby was different. She was the sexiest woman he'd ever met. She affected him in a way he couldn't control and he certainly didn't understand.

His eyes still shut, he felt her rise off his lap. When he opened them with curiosity, he saw that she had taken a place on the floor between his knees, her hands on his fly, unfastening the top button and lowering his zipper. He breathed a sigh of relief as he looked down at her, watching her every action, and he decided that he might not last long, but he was certain that he didn't want to miss a goddamn thing.

"Abby," he breathed, "this isn't necessary." His level head wanted him to be a gentleman, let her know that she needn't reciprocate, but he might scream in frustration if she backed away from him.

In response, she raised an eyebrow and put her hand inside his jeans and extracted his swollen dick from the denim.

She licked her lips and a saucy smirk crossed her lips. "What are *friends* for?" she whispered, before she edged over him, bringing him closer to her mouth.

Trevor held his breath when she leaned in and, with her tongue, captured the bead of moisture that had gathered at the tip. She shut her eyes and smiled, as if savoring the taste. She extended a wickedly long tongue and, starting at the base, she licked a line straight up the sensitive underside of his shaft until she reached the thick ridge of the head. She locked eyes with him as she opened her mouth and then closed her lips over him. He let go with a fully satisfied moan, every muscle in his body flexing and tensing under her touch and her power.

THRILLED BY TREVOR'S RESPONSE, Abby took him deeper in her mouth. She loved this part, this aspect of sex. She loved a man when he was completely at her mercy. When he focused on nothing but her. She took Trevor's incredible length deeper, and when she looked up at him, his eyes were open and on her. He was breathing deeply and had one hand clenched in the blanket on the couch, while his other hand landed on the back of her head. His fingers tangled in her hair and his grip was strong but his touch was light, urging her to take him deeper but not forcing her. He let her take control.

She moved her head up and down, her lips moving over him. She swirled her tongue over him, delighting in the silky skin contrasted with the solidness of him. Before long, his breath became short and raspy. And Abby could tell by the way his body tensed and the way he tightened his fist in her hair, pulling her lightly to him, that he was almost there.

His breathing increased, and he bucked his hips, thrusting into her mouth. But she went faster. His fingers released their hold of her hair and they spread cool across her flushed cheeks as he tried to push her away. "Abby, wait. I'm too close," he warned her.

She didn't listen. She removed his hands from her face, and she increased her pace.

"God. Abby, I'm—" But he couldn't finish his sentence. She felt him go stiff and then relax as he filled her mouth. Satisfied, she slowed her movements, gentling, and released him, backing away on her heels. She wiped the side of her mouth with her forefinger and crawled up on the couch, curling into his side while he stuffed his still semihard penis back into his pants.

His breathing was still heavy as he wrapped his arm around her. "That was amazing, Abby," Trevor said, shaking his head.

It pleased her but she kept her cool. "Don't I know it? You didn't do so poorly, yourself," she murmured, working to adjust her clothing. For the first time she noticed that the buttons of her shirt had been ripped clear from the fabric. She raised an eyebrow at him.

"Sorry," he laughed. "Let me get you a T-shirt. And, also, buy you a new blouse."

"I'd appreciate it. Thanks," she said as he got up and walked into his bedroom. She couldn't help but appreciate the view as he walked away. "Just remind me to go home and change next time if I'm coming over here straight from work."

10

TREVOR SAT BACK in his chair, raised his arms and locked his fingers behind his head. He watched Jamie as he read over the weekly and monthly numbers for the club. By the way his friend's eyebrows rose and how his smile made his lips twitch, Trevor knew that Jamie was impressed. Swerve Montreal had had a couple of killer months, more than doubling sales from the previous years, and they had received many fantastic reviews on online forums.

Jamie finally looked up, smiled at Trevor and closed the laptop. "Trev, man. The numbers are just great here. You're outperforming every other bar in the area and the rest of the Swerve locations in the country. Reviews are all great, and these numbers—" he held out the reports in his hand "—they speak for themselves. I don't know what you're doing here, man, but keep it up. I could use another you at every other bar. I've been getting some reports of inconsistencies and bartending problems at some other locations. You know we can't have that."

Trevor took the compliment and gave a pleased but

modest shrug. "I know, consistency is key. And thanks, but it's not just me. We've got a good team here." He wondered what issues were happening at other clubs. He wanted to ask, but he didn't like to get into general business issues. He looked after Swerve's Montreal location and only that club.

"And it shows that you can't discount a great leader." Jamie pointed at Trevor. "I know, with you, my baby is in good hands."

"I'm assuming, in this case only, that Swerve is your baby and not Maya." Montreal was Jamie's first location and the one that was nearest to his heart. His office headquarters were even located on the floors above them at the club.

Jamie laughed. "Yes. In this case only will I refer to Swerve as my baby, and she is the only one who will be in your hands, never Maya. But in all seriousness, you're great at what you do, man. You're one hell of a bartender, but you really know how to manage this place. And that is why I have this for you."

Jamie reached into his messenger bag and pulled out an envelope. He handed it to Trevor, who took it apprehensively. "What's this?"

Jamie sat back nonchalantly as Trevor lifted the flap of the envelope. "It's just a little token of appreciation, a bonus, for all of the good work you've done here."

Jamie pulled out the check and his eyes widened at the numbers written on it. Shock made him speechless for a moment before he put it on his desk and slid it back to Jamie. "I can't take that. It's too much."

Jamie pushed it back in Trevor's direction. "Stop it. Take it. You're worth one hundred times that amount. The company is doing well, and you're a big part of the reason why. You've been with me since the very beginning and I don't think I could have done any of this without you."

Knowing that Jamie would not relent, and knowing that the cash would certainly help with getting his own bar up and ready, Trevor picked up the check again. The number surprised him but he knew that the money could be put to good use. Swerve was doing well, and Trevor did work his ass off every day. He should just accept it. "I appreciate it, Jamie." He nodded and put the check in the top drawer. "Thank you."

"Thanks for actually taking it. I thought I'd have to physically fight you." Jamie looked around the office at the piles of paper and boxes and everything else that was scattered messily about the room. He shook his head. "Dude, your office is a mess."

"You know that's how I work." Trevor shrugged his shoulders. "Messy office, clean bar. If I cleaned up in here, how would I find anything when I need it?"

"How do you find anything now?" Jamie was skeptical.

Trevor surveyed his surroundings, feeling confident. "Anything I could possibly need in this office, I can put my hands on it, almost immediately."

"Really?"

"Try me." Trevor folded his arms across his chest, up for the challenge.

"Okay." Jamie tented his fingers in front of his face, thinking. "What if I needed to see the order form from Eight Bells Brewery?"

"Which month?" Trevor smiled, challenging Jamie.

Working his jaw, Jamie thought about it, an attempt to trick Trevor, no doubt. "August."

"August…" He stood and went over to a bookshelf across the room. He tapped his fingers on the shelf before him. He pulled a folder from a box and, with a sure smirk, he turned around to Jamie and handed him the file containing the order form he'd requested.

Jamie looked it over and rolled his eyes. "You got lucky. What about the most current building inspection report?"

Without a word or hesitation, Trevor pulled it from the bottom drawer of his desk and handed it to Jamie.

Jamie didn't even look at the papers in the folder. "Fine," he laughed. "Do whatever you want in here. You don't need me to tell you how to live your life. You've clearly got it under control in this place."

Trevor walked over to the mini fridge that he kept in his office. The business talk was out of the way; now he and his friend could relax with a drink. Trevor had watched Jamie change over the past months. Whereas Jamie was once a workaholic, he was now able to compartmentalize his life. Work was no longer his sole focus. And it was nice to have his friend back. He took out two bottles of beer and handed one to Jamie. "So, how does it feel to be betrothed?"

"Thanks." Jamie cracked open the seal and swallowed. He smiled at Trevor. "It's awesome. I get to see Maya every day, and I keep feeling like I'm falling more and more in love with her every time I look at her. I know we moved really quickly with the engagement, but you know what? It was the best decision I ever made."

"I'm glad. It's nice to see you happy. You look so relaxed."

"I feel relaxed. No matter what's going on with work, I just go home to Maya at the end of the day.

And she reminds me that I've hired a pretty talented team to look after things. I've got her to center me. Do you know what I mean?"

Trevor nodded. He remained silent. He really had no idea what it was like. Sure, he saw Abby almost every night, but she was steadfast in her refusal to have an actual relationship. He thought about what Jamie had just said, and he felt a longing for even just a minuscule fraction of what Jamie had described.

Jamie broke through his thoughts. "But how are you? You seeing anyone these days?"

That moment seemed like just as good of a time as any to tell Jamie. He had no reason to lie as they had shared intimate details of their personal lives pretty frequently in the past. "Well, I've been sort of seeing Abby."

Jamie didn't respond for a while, and then his brows furrowed. "Abby? Abby Shaw? Maya's best friend?"

Trevor nodded.

"You've been seeing Abby? Are you guys dating or something?"

Trevor took a pull from his beer and carefully selected his words. "*Something.* Well, we're not actually dating, per se. But we have been—I guess you could say *hooking up* a bit as of late."

"What does that even mean?" Jamie laughed. "You guys are sleeping together?"

"Yeah," he replied simply, putting his beer down and, leaning back in his chair again, he locked his fingers behind his head.

Jamie dragged his fingers through his own hair. "How did this come about? Does Maya know?"

"I don't know if Abby told her or not. We've been keeping it pretty low-key."

"She's pretty hot." Jamie nodded appreciatively. Trevor knew that Jamie only had eyes for Maya, and, even though he had no claim to Abby, he was annoyed that Jamie had noticed her at all. "So, how's the sex?" Jamie asked.

"Dude," Trevor reprimanded him with a glare. "Come on."

"*Come on*, what? It's not like we've never shared the nitty-gritty details before," Jamie protested.

"And, as I recall, you weren't exactly forthcoming about your relationship with Maya. Hell, even though I had some idea, I found out with the rest of the world when that video of you guys went up on the internet." Trevor immediately regretted bringing up the video that had surfaced of Jamie and Maya, which caught them in an intimate moment, embarrassing both of them and almost driving them apart.

Jamie frowned. "Trevor, I'm going to marry Maya. You know the rules. You don't talk about the stuff you do with the woman you're serious about." He stopped and looked at Trevor. "Unless it *is* serious with you and Abby."

Trevor said nothing and again drank his beer, ignoring Jamie's stare.

"Huh," Jamie said, thoughtfully. "Well, then. How long exactly has this relationship been going on?"

"It's not a relationship. And it's complicated." Trevor frowned, as he searched for the right words. But he just went with how he felt. "The truth? The truth is, I really want her. I think I always have. And being with her is amazing. But, God, I'm getting older and I don't know if it's watching you with Maya, but I feel like it's time to settle down. It feels like the sex just isn't enough, you know? Abby wants nothing to do with me—besides friendship and my amazing body and extraordinary prowess between the sheets, that is," he said wryly. "Apparently, she's given up on dating and relationships."

"Really?" Jamie asked.

"Yeah. She's convinced herself that relationships are bad and she doesn't want some guy falling in love with her or holding her back. And she wants to focus on her career."

Trevor was silent for a moment, thinking about the words he had to say next. If there was one person he could trust with his secret, it was Jamie. "I guess now is as good a time as any to tell you this—I'm leaving Swerve."

"What?" Jamie's bottle stopped midway to his mouth.

"Want that bonus check back?"

"Of course not. You've earned it. What's going on? You're really leaving?"

"Not today or anytime soon. I'll obviously wait until we have a new manager hired and trained, but I just wanted to let you know that—" he took a deep breath "—I'm opening my own bar." Trevor told Jamie about buying Shanahan's and the courses he was taking at the college. "It's time for me to get serious, start forging my own path."

Jamie said nothing for a while. But then he smiled. "That's awesome, Trev. I'm really happy for you. As your boss, I would obviously like to keep you here forever, but, as your friend, I know that you need to move on. I'm proud of you. I know you'll do great. Do you need any help with anything? Filling out the paperwork? Making a business plan? Money?"

"No, I definitely don't need money. I've got some saved, and you've already given me enough." He gestured to the drawer where he'd put the bonus check. "But I might need some advice from time to time."

"You got it. Anything you need, it's yours."

"Thanks, I appreciate that."

"So, where is it?" he asked. "I want to get in there. See the place."

"When are you free?"

Jamie consulted his phone. "How about the day after tomorrow? I've got some time in the evening."

"Sounds good to me," Trevor agreed.

Jamie extended his bottle, and he knocked it against Trevor's. "I'm really happy for you, man. And congratulations. It's going to be great."

"You and Trevor are *what*?"

Abby looked around the crowded restaurant. Some faces were pointed in the direction of the table she shared with Maya, in reaction to Maya's exclamation at the news that Abby had just dropped on her. "Maya, keep it down please. We're in public."

Abby and Maya had spent the morning and afternoon in bridal salons, Maya trying on wedding dresses and Abby trying not to cry at how beautiful her best friend looked in each one. Eventually, after trying on dozens of white, ivory and champagne-colored dresses, Maya finally found *the one*, so the two were having a celebratory lunch.

"Fine," Maya whispered, leaning in. "You and Trevor are what?"

"We're hooking up," Abby repeated, waving a dismissive hand, taking a sip from her mojito. *Good. Not as good as Trevor can make*, she thought with a small smile. "It's really not that big of a deal."

"Trevor is Jamie's best friend." Maya's eyes were wide as she recounted each fact. "And you're my best friend. And you guys are dating. This is crazy."

"It's not so crazy," Abby explained. "And we're not dating. We're just two good friends who hang out."

"And have sex," Maya supplied.

"And have sex. Yes."

They didn't hear the waiter approach, who had obviously overheard at least part of their conversation. With a small smile, he put their plates in front of them—Maya's salad and Abby's burger with fries. "Enjoy, ladies," he muttered quietly before making a hasty retreat.

"Thank you," Maya called out to him before returning to the matter at hand. "But what about the whole being-done-with-relationships thing?"

Abby dipped a French fry in a cup of chipotle mayo and popped it into her mouth. "This is delish," she declared and she pushed her plate toward her friend. "Want one?"

Maya shook her head adamantly. "I have to fit into that gorgeous white dress that I just spent way too much money on, remember? I'm fine with my salad."

Abby nodded. "Well, that's the thing. I realized that just because I'm no longer in the market for a boyfriend, it doesn't mean that I can't just have sex with a gorgeous guy when the mood strikes me. And Trevor is definitely a gorgeous guy."

Maya cast a critical gaze on her friend. "And what if, through some crazy happenstance, you start to develop feelings for him?"

"It's never gonna happen," she said, emphatically.

"Well, what if he wants more from you?"

Abby shook her head. "Don't worry. We laid out the ground rules early on. Nobody is falling in love with anybody else. Nobody's feelings will be hurt. It's just physical," Abby emphasized. "Everything is going to be fine."

Maya shook her head. "I don't know. You know how it was with me and Jamie," she said. "That kind of desire always gets out of control."

"That was you and Jamie, and you are meant for each other. Not to mention that whole secret, forbidden affair. That's why you guys couldn't keep your hands off each other. You are soul mates and all that. Trevor and I are just friends." Abby shrugged before picking up her burger and taking a bite. She swallowed and then turned back to Maya. "Trevor and I are friends. That's all," she repeated.

Maya still wasn't convinced. "Jamie and I didn't know we were *meant for each other*, as you say," Maya said. "All we knew is that when we were in the same room we needed to see who could undress the other more quickly. So, if your situation isn't like that, you'll probably be fine."

Abby stopped, midchew, and she considered Trevor. If he were around at that very moment, she would have absolutely no second thoughts about stripping off all of his clothes and having sex with him on the table before her, right in the middle of the restaurant. If she was being honest, Abby would admit that since they started sleeping together, whenever they were together, with only a couple of exceptions, they ended up naked within minutes. She looked at Maya and huffed out a heavy breath. There was nothing for her to say.

"Is it like that with you and Trevor?" Maya asked her, one eyebrow raised high.

Abby was sure that Maya already knew the answer. "Maybe. But that doesn't mean anything," Abby maintained. "We have strong sexual chemistry. Hormones. We're just having fun."

"If you say so," Maya said with a shrug and returned to her salad.

But Abby put down her burger and drained the rest of the mojito in her glass. She *was* wildly attracted to Trevor. But was she developing feelings for him? She shook her head. *No!* She couldn't be. She wasn't about to let herself fall in love with Trevor Jones.

_11_

"ABBY?"

She looked up from her computer at François as he called to her from the conference room across the office. She watched as every head between her and their boss swiveled in her direction. _Nosy bunch._

"Yes?"

"Can I see you for a moment?" The toothy smile that normally rested on François's face was gone, replaced by the firm, straight line of his lips. Whatever he wanted to see her about wasn't good.

"Yeah, sure." She stood, her voice shaky at his forceful tone. Her coworkers went back to their work as she made her way to the conference room and she closed the door behind her. "Is something wrong?" she asked as she took a seat across the table from her boss.

"Well, Abby, I just heard from Ashbourne and they're a little concerned about the proposal that you submitted to them."

Abby's cautious smile faded. "What? Why?"

François slid the folder, which she assumed contained

her proposal, across the table. "They are concerned about your work."

Abby mouth dropped and she felt everything come tumbling down around her. "What specifically are their concerns?" She took the folder and opened it. And then she saw it, highlighted on the first page. The name of Ashbourne's CEO, Sylvie Poulin, was highlighted in yellow and she had somehow spelled it *Putain*, a very crass French-Canadian curse word.

"Oh, *mon Dieu*," Abby whispered and brought a shocked hand to her mouth. "Oh my God," she said, this time louder, switching back to her native tongue. She looked up at François and saw a small smile playing on his lips. "I can't believe I did that. I'm so sorry."

François winked and smiled broadly. "I'm sorry for the pretense. I'm just having a little fun with you."

"François!" Abby exclaimed, mortified. "So, I'm not fired or off the project?"

"No, of course not," he assured her. "It's an unfortunate mistake, Abby. One you won't make again, correct?" Abby nodded furiously. "And Sylvie thought it was quite funny. As you can imagine, it isn't the first time she's seen it."

Abby buried her face in her hands. She couldn't believe that she had made such a mistake on her first really big account. "How do I fix this?"

"It isn't a big deal. At least they caught it before it went out in a press release. But, Abby, we really do need you to demonstrate a little more care in the future. It's only a small mistake, but something like that could really derail your career."

"Of course, I'll be more careful. I still can't believe it. I need to call her to apologize." She looked up at François across the table. "Is there anything else?"

"No, you're free to go." He took in her shaken appearance. "You do really good work, Abby, and you're a strong member of the team. We all do things like this sometimes. Don't worry about it too much."

Abby nodded and stood. "Thank you," she mumbled. Walking out of the room, she kept her head lowered, evading the confused, concerned stares of her coworkers. She replayed François's words over in her head.

Don't worry about it too much.

How could she not worry about the fact that she had basically called the CEO of Ashbourne Cosmetics a *whore*? She sat at her desk. She opened her email, about to send a message apologizing to everyone at Ashbourne for her terrible mistake, when her cell phone vibrated on her desk next to her elbow. She picked it up and unlocked the screen. It was a text message from Trevor.

Want to get together tonight?

She totally did. Abby *definitely* needed to work off a little tension with Trevor. And soon.

Sure. What time?

I'll be tied up until around 6:30.

Sounds good. Come over to my place.

I'll be there.

Abby smiled at the way they arranged a booty call as if it were a business meeting. But she was relieved. A night with Trevor would more than relieve her of all of the stress from her terrible mistake.

She looked down at the file with the curse word highlighted in yellow and frowned. She couldn't believe that something like that would have happened. She was normally so careful.

But wasn't that what she was afraid of happening the minute she got involved with a man? That he would distract her from her work? Sure, she wasn't dating Trevor, but here she was nonetheless, apologizing to her client for misspelling her name in the worst way possible.

Like François had said, it was only an interdepartmental document, not part of a press release or anything. But that didn't stop her from feeling like an idiot. This would probably be her legacy. From here on out, she would be known as the woman who had inadvertently called a high-profile client a whore.

Maybe she should just end things with Trevor. Maybe he was far too great a distraction for her. Maybe she should just call it quits on their arrangement. She looked at her phone.

After tonight.

12

ABBY GASPED FOR air and fell forward onto the mattress with a satisfied sigh before Trevor fell on top of her, his chest to her back. He wrapped his arms around her waist and rolled over to lie on his back, pulling her to his side.

She delighted in the warmth from his body and smiled contentedly. If she was interested in pursuing a relationship with Trevor—which she wasn't—she could definitely get used to this. "What time is it?"

Abby had left work early and had called Trevor on her way home. He met her at her door, and they had barely made it to her bedroom before they were naked and entwined. Their clothes, no doubt, littered her apartment.

Trevor consulted his watch, the only thing he was still wearing. "Almost nine," he pronounced.

"Wow," she said, amazed. "Where did this evening go?"

Trevor chuckled and the deep sound made her shiver. "I think that nearly empty box of condoms can tell you how we lost all of that time."

"Is it empty? I just bought those!"

He shrugged. "There's one left. I guess you're going to have to make a trip to Costco. Get one of those giant boxes. Make sure we're covered."

Abby laughed. She wasn't sure that even Costco could keep her in prophylactics as long as she was dating—*no, not dating!*—Trevor.

He looked over at her. "So, how was your day?"

She laughed, no longer feeling the stress that she'd felt earlier in the day. "Well, it was interesting," she began and then told him what had happened with the Sylvie Poulin.

When she finished, Trevor laughed. "That's unfortunate. How did you manage to do that?"

"I don't know. Just an honest mistake, I guess. It was pretty embarrassing, though, even if *some people*—" she smacked him lightly on the chest "—think it's funny."

They lay there in silence for a few moments.

"I'm sorry I laughed," Trevor said.

"It's okay. Everything is fine now. My boss thought it was hilarious, and I groveled to Ashbourne's CEO. She understood that it was an accident. She was very nice about it." She paused. "I guess I was just…distracted." That was it. Abby was going to tell Trevor that she couldn't see him anymore. She couldn't afford any more mistakes like the one she had already made. She tried to find the words, but she came up blank.

Abby looked up at Trevor. His strong arms surrounded her, and she felt his warmth surround her. Using her fingers, she traced the lines of the tattoos that covered his right arm. "What do your tattoos mean?"

"What makes you think they mean anything?" he asked her.

Abby knew he wasn't the type of guy to permanently transform his body solely for aesthetic reasons. There was more to Trevor than that. He was deeper. "Because I don't think that many people go through the time and pain, not to mention the cost, of covering so much of their body with ink if it doesn't mean anything."

"You've got me there. What about your ink?" he asked her, lightly slapping the small butterfly above her ass. "What's that butterfly about?"

"That was a dumb idea after too many margaritas when I was nineteen," she laughed, rolling her eyes. "Maya has one, too. We were young and impulsive."

Trever laughed. "It's pretty cute, though."

Abby went back to regarding the artwork carefully, how the different images all swirled and transitioned into others. She had never before noticed how intricate and beautiful the black and grayscale designs were. She traced one high on his shoulder.

"This Celtic cross—an homage to your Irish roots?"

"That's right. My grandparents immigrated when my father was a baby."

She pointed to an image that was almost bird-like. Its head and wings upturned, as if it was flying from a pile of rubble. The image covered the majority of his upper arm. It was beautiful, complex. She ran her fingers over it. "What about this one? What's this?"

Trevor hesitated for a moment and she thought that she may have overstepped by asking about his tattoos. It was a very personal, intimate topic, but they were currently lying naked in bed, limbs intertwined. She didn't think that it got much more intimate than that.

"A phoenix," he responded simply.

"Like the mythical creature?"

"Yeah."

Abby recalled some mythology courses she'd taken during her undergraduate degree.

"The phoenix rises from the ashes. Symbolizes strength, rebirth, change?"

He nodded.

"What does it mean to you?"

"It was one of my first tattoos." He paused before continuing. "I was eighteen. It felt like I was stuck at the time. After my grandmother passed away, I was responsible for looking after myself and my little brother, Will. We weren't very well-off. I managed to get a job at a bar and I quickly worked my way from bar back to managing the place. And eventually I was making enough money to support us both. I basically came from nothing and I did well for myself, and this tattoo was my way of marking how I'd started over. Rising from the proverbial ash of a shitty, dysfunctional childhood and becoming a man."

Abby smiled at him. She admired his story. Trevor was such a strong and proud man, and he had done well for himself. She grasped his hand and turned it so that the lioness etched into the bottom side of his forearm was revealed. "What about this one? A female lion?"

Trevor took another deep breath, and Abby wondered if she was taxing him by asking such personal questions. But she couldn't stop. It seemed that, with every sentence he spoke, she liked him more and she needed to know more about him. "That one is for my grandmother."

"What was she like?"

"She was an amazing woman." Abby could see the memory of her alighting his eyes. "She took us in when our father died. She was kind and loving, but she was strong. Fierce, almost. She was a tough woman who had gone through too much. I remember learning that the female lions are the ones who look after the pride. Keep everyone in line, make sure there's food for everyone, the pride is protected and the young ones don't get into any trouble," he finished with a smile. "I figured it would be a nice tribute."

Abby smiled. "She sounds wonderful."

"She was."

She felt Trevor's arms tighten around her waist. She knew that he was done talking about his past. She was worried that she had opened a gate where he would start asking her questions. Luckily, he looked at her with a saucy smile.

"Well, I think that's about enough introspection for tonight. But seeing as how we're almost out of protection, what do you think we should do with the rest of the evening?"

"There are things we can do that don't require protection."

"That's true. As much as I enjoy hanging out in bed with you, I was thinking maybe we could go out somewhere."

"Yeah?"

"Well, we could go out and get a late dinner, maybe go to a movie?"

"Dinner and a movie?" she asked him skeptically. "That sounds like something a couple would do."

"Well, we're a *couple* of friends."

"It sounds like a date." Abby shook her head.

"We've gone out to eat together before. We've seen movies together. We've been out together lots of times," he reminded her.

It felt like a lifetime had passed since they'd started sleeping together. "It was different then."

"Okay, it would be a date, then. Would that be so bad?" he whispered against her temple, before kissing her lightly. "For us to go out on a date or something like that?"

She stiffened in his arms at the question. She frowned. "It's against the rules that we both agreed to. You know that isn't allowed."

Trevor withdrew his arms from her, letting her fall away from her perch at his side. "Apparently not," he muttered.

She'd hurt him. She knew it and she felt bad about it. She inched closer to him and reached out to touch him. "Trevor…"

"No, it's fine. You're right," he said. Even though he was still close to her, she could feel the distance put between them by his tone and body language. "I'm sorry. We agreed not to make this any more than it is."

"You have to understand. It's not about you. You're great—"

"I understand," he interrupted her, warming again. He rolled to his side, facing her. He wrapped his hand around her waist and pulled her closer to him. "How about we just order a pizza and then we grab that last condom and get back to doing something that is within the well-established, agreed-upon parameters of our nonrelationship?"

13

TREVOR STOOD NEXT to Jamie on the sidewalk in front of the shuttered bar. "You bought Shanahan's?" Jamie turned to him as Trevor unlocked the door. Trevor simply nodded.

"The bar you bought without telling anyone is Shanahan's? I can't believe it. I didn't even know this place was on the market," he said.

Trevor followed him in and pulled the dusty tarpaulin from the top of the bar, exposing the original wood of the surface. After hearing about Trevor's purchase of the bar, Jamie had insisted he see it before he and Maya headed back to Las Vegas.

"Look at this thing. It's incredible." Jamie ran his hand over the smooth but worn surface. "This place hasn't changed at all—well, except for the five or six layers of accumulated dust."

"I know. I wanted it to be a surprise until I got her all fixed up," Trevor said, turning on the lights. "But since you wouldn't let it go until you saw it… I'm going to rename it, of course, and rebrand, but I hope to keep some of the same charm the place always had."

"I'm glad you showed me." Jamie looked around the room. "Man, it's been ages since I've set foot in this place."

When Trevor looked around the room, he was transported back to when he had just graduated from high school and his grandmother had suffered a stroke and passed away. His grades had been decent enough to earn him scholarships to some good colleges, but he had to put that on hold to support himself and his younger brother. And he gladly did it. He was the man of the house, after all, and he had to look after his family. It was his responsibility—a trait his grandmother, not his own father, had instilled in him. So Trevor went to work, imagining that there would be time later to go back to school. But back then he hadn't realized that *putting it on hold* would mean thirteen years.

Trevor watched Jamie survey the space, and he knew that his friend was reflecting on the same memories that Trevor was. Shanahan's was where he had first met Jamie when they were both eighteen-year-old punk kids, lying about their age so they could work there, just to earn a living. Their paths diverged with Jamie going to college and becoming a mogul and Trevor staying on at the bar, but no matter how different their lives had turned out, they remained close friends. They were both quiet for a moment, thinking about the past.

"So, when are you planning to open?" Jamie asked finally, breaking the silence. His hands were on his hips as he looked around. Trevor knew that he was in business-mode. Jamie knew the bar business like no other, and he seemed to be checking out the space with a critical eye, identifying all of the strengths and weaknesses of the place and the opportunities that Trevor had before him.

He had been hoping to finish his short school program before he opened. "I'm not sure yet. I bought the place now because the price was right and I didn't want to risk losing it to someone else. But I don't want to do anything until I know it's ready. Plus, I haven't finished with my classes yet, although I'm not sure I can leave it shuttered for very long before I start losing money."

"Don't wait too long." Jamie turned to him. "If you really want to wait until you're done with school, that's fine. It's your timeline. But I don't think you need to. If there's one thing you know, it's the bar business. You could open and run this place with your eyes closed."

"I know that," Trevor admitted. "And I just might. But I went back to school because it felt like something I *needed* to do, you know?"

Jamie nodded. "I do. I know you gave up a lot to help your grandmother and your brother." He paused. "But enough of the feelings and all that bullshit." He smiled, still scoping out the bar. "This is going to be great."

"I hope so." Trevor crossed his arms and leaned against the wall behind the bar.

"I mean it," Jamie insisted "This place is definitely special, and I'm sure it's missed in the neighborhood. I know I told you this before, but if you need any help with anything, and I mean *anything*, let me know and it's yours."

"Thanks." Trevor knew that he would have Jamie's support. But he didn't want to take anything else from him. This was something he needed to do on his own. He needed to prove to himself and everyone else that he was serious and responsible enough to pull it off.

14

WITH HIS LIFE full of distractions as of late—his job at Swerve, his new bar and Abby—Trevor had some catching up to do on the schoolwork that he had been neglecting. That afternoon, Robin had texted him to see if he wanted to get together to work on an assignment that was due the next day and, knowing that he couldn't put it off any longer, Trevor agreed to meet her at her place to work on it.

He watched Robin across the table from him. He still wasn't quite sure what her intentions were. She was flirtatious and sexy. He wasn't interested in her romantically. She was way too young for him. But it was nice to have a classmate, a friend in the program, no matter their differences. And then, of course, he had to consider what he had going on with Abby, wherever he stood with her.

Trevor watched Robin as she skimmed over lines in her textbook and input numbers into her calculator. "I'm never going to get this," Robin said, sighing as she threw her forehead down on her textbook. "It's useless. I'm a lost cause."

"It's not that bad," Trevor said. He took her book from her. "Look, we can get this done. We just have one more question and then we'll be finished with this assignment." *And I can go home*, Trevor thought. He hadn't made any plans with Abby that night, but he might shoot her a quick text later to see if she wanted to get together.

Robin looked at her watch and Trevor also looked at his. It was after eleven thirty and he could barely keep his eyes open. Maybe he wouldn't be texting Abby later, after all. She was definitely in bed at this late hour. But he couldn't tamp down the disappointment he felt at the thought of not seeing her.

He yawned. If he was still working behind the bar, his night would just be getting started and he would have a few hours left to his shift. But since he'd started working daytime hours, his sleep schedule had regulated and he'd found himself in bed most nights by midnight.

"God," Robin whined as she pounded some more numbers into her calculator. "I know it was my idea to get together to finish this thing, but I'm officially over it. It's so boring!"

"Come on," he said. "It's not that bad. We shouldn't be too much longer."

"Trevor, I know that school is important and an education is so valuable. I get it. But we're young and we should be out having fun, instead of having to do this stupid assignment. When will we ever use this stuff?" She gestured at the book in frustration.

Trevor smiled at the young woman and her whining. Of course she couldn't see at that point in her life where it would come in handy to know anything about financial management. But he could already think of examples in which he would use the formulas he was learning in the class. Sure, it was tough and it was definitely dull, but he was glad he was doing it. It would serve him well.

"It might come up. Any day now," he said, laughing, and removed her book from under her face.

"Doubtful." She sighed. She got up and walked into her kitchen. She rustled about for a minute or so. When she returned, she was holding an opened bottle of wine and two glasses. She sat back at the table, scooted her chair closer to him and poured them each a glass.

With trepidation, Trevor eyed the glass of red wine she'd pushed in front of him. "I don't think I should. I've got my motorcycle." He noticed the way Robin was watching him and tried to figure out if she was coming on to him.

She shrugged. "Fine. If you don't want any, that's more for me." She picked up his glass and drank from it before returning her attention to her textbook, and she breathed out a huff of frustration that caught his attention. He watched Robin as she tapped her pencil against her full lips. A subconscious action or a carefully plotted form of seduction, drawing his attention to them? Trevor pulled his eyes away from her and tried to read from the textbook. But his gaze was brought back to her when she traced the pencil along her jawline and then down to her cleavage, exposed by the low-cut V of her shirt's neckline.

Trevor picked up his calculator and focused on inputting the numbers from the assignment's last question. He cleared his throat. Robin was a beautiful girl; younger than he would normally go for, she was only twenty-one, but with her previous flirtations, the wine and then her body language, he knew for sure that she was coming on to him.

It couldn't happen with her. There was no way. He had to focus on school and not the young woman before him. And then there was Abby and their current non-relationship relationship. Even though they weren't officially a couple, being with another woman definitely felt like it would be a betrayal.

Robin leaned over her chair, apparently reaching for something in her bag. Her forehead brushed the side of his thigh. Trevor put up his hands. He had to put an end to this. *Now.*

He cleared his throat. "Robin, this can't happen."

She sat up abruptly, puzzled. "Why? What answer did you get?" She looked at his notepaper, checking his answer.

"No, Robin, I'm not talking about the assignment. This can't happen, between us." He sat back, putting a firm hand between them.

"What are you talking about?"

"The wine, the way you're acting. You're coming on to me, and we can't do this."

"Hmm…" She bit her lip, cutting off her smile. "And why not, exactly?"

"Because," he said, trying to find a way to explain his reasons. "I just can't. There's school, I'm trying to get a business off the ground and I just don't have time for another relationship at this point in my life."

She was quiet for a beat. "Wait, *another* relationship?" She had latched on to the one word he hadn't even meant to say. "I didn't know you were seeing anybody."

"What?" he asked.

"You said that you didn't have time for *another rela-tionship*. And I said that I didn't know you were seeing anybody. I've never heard you mention another girl."

"I didn't say... I'm not—" He struggled, suddenly embarrassed and regretting that he'd even said any-thing. "Never mind. I should go."

Robin laughed at him. "Well, look at you, Trevor Jones." She picked up her glass and watched him over the rim. "All tied up in knots about this. Who's the other woman?"

"There is no other woman. There's nobody. I've got to go." He stood, gathering his things.

Robin put a hand on his textbook, which kept him from picking it up. "Trevor, don't worry. Your virtue is safe with me. You know, you aren't exactly my type."

Trevor paused. "So, wait just a minute here," he started. "If you aren't coming on to me, what exactly is your type?"

"Well, I like 'em tall, blond hair, gorgeous, mus-cles... Like my boyfriend..." She trailed off.

"What?"

"I have a boyfriend, Trevor," she explained. "Is that so hard to believe? He lives in Vancouver. He's going to school there. I swear, I wasn't coming on to you. I mean, sure, you're good-looking and all, but I don't cheat. And plus, you're also kind of ancient. You're *way* older than I am."

Trevor frowned. So, his radar was *definitely* off. He had mistaken Robin's friendliness for sexual interest. "I'm sorry. That's embarrassing," he said, laughing. "I can't believe that just happened. I thought I had to lay down the law here."

"I know," Robin said. "How egotistical are you? Not every woman who talks to you wants to jump your bones, Trevor. Don't worry about it." She smiled and put a hand on his arm. She retracted it quickly, a falsely horrified look on her face. "Oh, God, I'm sorry. That wasn't me coming on to you again." She rolled her eyes at him dramatically and sipped her wine.

"But why don't you tell me about this girl who's got you so tangled up that you can't let a very attractive classmate—me—try to take advantage of you by plying you with wine?"

She surprised him. Robin was sharper than she seemed. "It's nothing," he stated and picked up the assignment page. He wasn't about to let Robin in on his arrangement with Abby and let her dissect his life and his romantic feelings for the friend he was currently sleeping with.

She watched him closely. "I don't think I quite believe you, Trevor."

"Let's just finish up this assignment, why don't we?" he pleaded.

"Fine," Robin huffed and returned to her notebook. "If you insist. God, why couldn't you find me irresistible? If you did, then homework would be the last thing on your mind."

Trevor laughed, and he knew that he would never live down that transgression. He went back to his work. Or at least he tried to. But he thought about Abby instead, and he must have read the same page fifteen times before he gave up. He sighed. "It isn't a relationship."

She looked up from her work. "What's not a relationship?"

"What we were talking about earlier. I am seeing someone, but it's definitely not a relationship." He wasn't sure why he was telling her this. Maybe he just needed to get it all out. Maybe Robin could help him. Shed a little light on the female perspective.

"Okay."

"We're sleeping together, but she doesn't want to see me outside of the bedroom." He let out a frustrated breath.

Robin smiled. "Got yourself a little *fuck buddy*, eh?" She giggled.

He ignored her and carried on. "And when I suggested going out on the simplest of nondates, she shot me down completely. We made these rules saying that we could sleep together, hang out as friends, but nothing else."

Robin considered his predicament and chewed her bottom lip. "Well, do you want more than that?"

Trevor thought about it. He did want more with Abby. "Yeah."

"Well, look at you, Trevor," Robin said. "You're in love with her, aren't you?"

"No," Trevor replied emphatically. "I like her. A lot. But it's definitely not love."

"No?"

He hesitated.

Robin nodded and a frustratingly knowing smile passed over her lips. "Of course not. Well, Trevor, if you want this girl, don't scare her away. She's obviously afraid of commitment. Or she has some trust issues or whatever. Just win her over. Just be smooth. Don't make any grand gestures. And don't rush her. Give her all the time she needs." She paused to let her words sink in. "And she likes you well enough to sleep with you. Women don't usually take that kind of thing too lightly. Just give her what she wants, and if that's just your studly self, then that's what you offer her until she comes around…which she probably will, if you give her time. Let her know what a great guy you are."

Trevor said nothing. Then he nodded at her. "That's pretty good advice. Thanks, Robin."

"Anytime you need my expertise, just ask." She smiled at him.

At that moment, Trevor decided, that's what he would do. He would win over Abby Shaw.

15

ABBY STEPPED OUTSIDE her office building and felt the sun caress her face. Abby had worked through most of her lunch break, so she took a few minutes before her next meeting with the team from Ashbourne to pop into the coffee shop next to her office building for a caffeine boost.

Her long days at work and her even longer nights with Trevor were starting to take their toll on her functionality. She was constantly exhausted and she used most of her concealer to cover the dark circles that lack of sleep had brought underneath her eyes. But she wasn't about to cut back on either work or Trevor. So caffeinating herself to the point where she was jittery seemed like her only option to get through her days.

She was just leaving the café, quad-shot of espresso in her hand, when she heard the unmistakeable, powerful roar of a motorcycle approaching. Since she'd started seeing Trevor, Abby had developed a habit of turning her head whenever she heard a motorcycle approach, thinking, *hoping*, that it might be Trevor. It hardly ever was; there were hundreds, if not *thousands*, of motorcycles in the city. But the gray, black and chrome beast roaring toward her was indeed familiar.

The machine pulled into the café parking lot, and stopped, partially obscured behind a delivery van. Abby stood and watched. The driver dismounted before removing his helmet, but she knew it was Trevor. Everything about him and his body, the way he moved, was familiar to her and sent a rush of heat through her chest and then straight to her core. She watched him remove his helmet, and she was about to head over to say hello, when she saw the woman seated on the back of the bike. The woman dismounted from the bike, taking off her own helmet and shaking her long brown hair free. Abby had never seen her before, had no idea who she was. Trevor had never mentioned seeing anyone else.

Abby quickly ducked behind a nearby SUV, out of sight of Trevor and the unidentified woman as she handed Trevor her helmet—she couldn't have been more than twenty-one or twenty-two—and then went inside the café, with Trevor holding the door for her, both of them smiling and laughing. Abby took a deep breath, drank some of her espresso and emerged from her hiding spot, frowning as, from outside, she watched them select a table near the huge front window and sit close together, placing coffee cups on the table. Abby rolled her eyes before moving on.

He can do whatever he likes, she decided. *It's not like you and Trevor are in a relationship or anything.* She had no claim on him. But she still couldn't discount the jolt of pain that pulled at her chest. Seeing him with another woman hit her squarely in the stomach and her breathing became shallow. She firmed her jaw and her hurt quickly turned to anger. She reviewed the rules in her head. They'd agreed to end their arrangement if either found someone else. Why didn't Trevor tell her he'd found someone? Maybe he had the same arrangement with this girl.

Abby downed her espresso and threw the cup in a nearby trash can. She huffed out a breath and stomped across the street. She opened the door to her office building. When an idea came to her, she smiled. She felt the challenge, and her competitive spirit rose. Whatever that other chick was giving Trevor, Abby decided that she could definitely do it better. Café girl was no competition to her at all. Abby's mind raced. She was going to give him a night he would never forget.

16

TREVOR WAS JUST getting out of the shower when he heard the loud knocking on his door. He frowned and, forgoing a shirt or even boxers, he quickly pulled on his most comfortable jeans, not bothering to fasten the top button, and walked to the door as the pounding on the door continued.

"I'm coming," he called with an impatient edge. He'd had a long day. First, school and then the club to take care of his responsibilities there. But there were several problems waiting for him when he got to Swerve. First, his assistant manager had noticed a problem with the schedule that Trevor had done, which left the coming Friday night understaffed. Then he saw that a delivery order had gotten mixed up, and he had to contend with the palette of tomatoes that had been delivered from a grocery distributor instead of the fruits and other assorted garnishes that he had actually ordered. After that fire was put out, he then had to balance three nights' worth of sales and deposits that had been done incorrectly, and he made arrangements to once again train his head bartenders to do it correctly.

In his absence, important details were getting missed and mistakes were being made. It seemed that Swerve was falling apart without him being there full-time to handle everything himself. He felt bad, especially since Jamie had earlier lamented about some problems at other locations and praised Trevor's contributions to keeping the flagship club running smoothly. Jamie depended on him and it seemed as if no one else could be trusted to do the things that Trevor normally handled.

He had spent several frustrating hours in his office that afternoon. Much longer than he'd expected. After that, he picked up Robin and they went to a coffee shop near her apartment to do a little more studying for their midterm the next morning. The last thing he had felt like doing was studying, but it was worth it. He finally felt prepared for the test and he looked forward to spending a quiet night at home with his television and a six-pack.

Was he stretching himself too thin? Between work, school and his extracurricular activities with Abby, he felt that something had to give. He had been so tired by the time he'd got home that he hadn't even texted Abby. He hadn't had the energy.

The ceaseless pounding on the other side of his door did nothing to calm his mood, and he feared that it greatly threatened his plans to do absolutely nothing for the rest of the night. When he got to his foyer, he sighed and opened the door with an annoyed "what?"

Even though he wasn't expecting her company, the person he saw on the other side surprised him pleasantly. It was Abby. They hadn't made plans and he'd been looking forward to some solitude, but did he mind that she was there? *No freakin' way.*

He looked her up and down, his fatigue and frustration quickly disappearing, replaced by lust and a renewed energy. He silently thanked God that he had studied for the next day's exam earlier with Robin because there was no way he could even think about his schoolwork or the nightclub with Abby standing in the doorway, looking how she looked.

She was wearing a short black trench coat, cinched tightly at her waist, and he wondered if she might be naked underneath. Her hair was mussed as if she'd already been properly sexed, and her makeup was a sultry palette of black and gray on her eyes and her lips were a deep red. Because he wasn't a fool, Trevor moved so that she could step inside. Without even a glance in his direction, she walked past him effortlessly on dangerously slim and high stiletto heels, which featured a sexy T-strap up the front of her foot and fastened in a little buckle at her ankle. He watched her saunter into his living room. She still hadn't spoken a word to him.

He folded his arms across his bare chest. "So, what brings you by this evening?" he asked. "I don't remember making plans to get together."

With her back still turned to him, Abby shrugged and undid the belt of her trench coat. He waited, holding his breath for what felt like an eternity before the coat dropped from her shoulders. His question was answered—while she was *not* naked underneath the jacket, she may as well have been because the lacy red bra and matching thong she wore didn't exactly cover her. He sucked in a breath, suddenly speechless. Then he laughed breathlessly.

Abby looked at him over her shoulder, her gaze hard. "What's so funny?"

"I thought for a second that you might not be wearing anything under that coat."

She laughed, as well. "What sort of complete cliché do you think I am? Am I the kind of woman who would come unannounced to a man's apartment wearing only high heels and a trench coat? You watch far too many movies, Trevor."

He went to her, her back still to him. Resting his hands on her hips, he leaned into her. "You are absolutely not a cliché," he whispered in her ear before dropping his mouth to her shoulder. "And you are nothing like any movie I've ever seen. You are original, amazing and I don't think I've ever *seen* a sexier woman."

He felt her relax against him. Her eyes closed when he put a palm flat on her leg and ran it up the smooth skin of her inner thigh. She hissed when his fingers found her, and they skimmed along the outside of the filmy material that barely covered her.

Trevor stroked her several times through her panties, her legs shifting wider as they stood in his living room. He pulled away quickly and smiled when he heard her sad whimper. His lips found the outer shell of her ear, and he was satisfied when she shivered as he whispered, "Why don't we take this into the bedroom?"

ABBY MOURNED THE absence of his clever fingers as soon as he pulled away from her. She had come to Trevor's house to show him that she could be hotter and more desirable than any woman he put on the back of his bike. But what she would never admit was that she also had to show herself that she could just take what she needed from him. A reminder to them both that their arrangement did not equate to a real relationship, no matter how greatly he affected her. No matter how much she wanted him every second of the day.

On her way home from work, she'd stopped into a lingerie boutique and found the red number that she was wearing, and she knew that it would drive him wild when paired with her sexiest shoes and the appropriate come-hither makeup. She knew just what to do to make an impression on him.

But the minute he'd answered the door in only a pair of unfastened jeans, hair wet, freshly showered, she realized that she was in danger of completely losing it. She wasn't sure where it was safe to look—at the strong arms, covered in tattoos; his pecs; those abs; the coarse hair that covered his chest and ran down his midline and disappeared behind the unbuttoned waistband of his worn jeans. Abby had to force herself to take a deep breath and stare straight ahead, turning her back on him so that she could properly seduce him without turning into a melty puddle at his bare feet. She needed to regain control of the situation. And she thought she could do it, too, but when he stepped near her, she smelled his body wash and shampoo and she inhaled deeply. When he touched her, she was gone. His masterful fingers strummed her through the small scrap of lace and it wasn't until he moved away from her that she even remembered why she was there.

He'd asked her about going into his bedroom, and she nodded. "Yeah, let's," she whispered and walked out of his reach, into his bedroom. She didn't have to turn around to know that he was following closely behind.

In the short walk to his bedroom, she took several deep breaths and managed to somehow regain her composure. Then she walked past his bed, stood against the far wall and folded her arms across her chest. The actions plumped up her cleavage in the low-cut of her bra, and she felt his eyes on her. "Seeing anything you like?"

"Seeing quite a few things that I like, actually," he responded, his gaze hot, traveling over her, scorching her body. She could feel the trail of his eyes burning into her skin. The heat in his stare made her shudder.

She could feel his ravenous hunger for her, but instead of succumbing to it, she felt empowered by his need. She looked at his bed, at the iron bars and the vertical wooden slats of his masculine, rustic headboard, and she felt a moment of inspiration. "Get on the bed," she ordered him.

His eyebrow arched. "Oh, really?"

She nodded. "Get on the bed." She turned and opened the thin, top drawer where she knew he kept the ties he so hated wearing, and she pulled out a thin, yellow silk tie and held it in her hands, weaving it through her fingers. When she turned back to the bed, she saw that he had followed her instructions and she smiled.

He was sitting on the bed, against the middle of the headboard, and he eyed the tie in her hands with the unmistakable fire of craving. "Where do you want me?"

Instead of answering him, she kneeled on the bed and slid toward him. "Lie down, head against the headboard." He nodded and leaned against it. She straddled his narrow waist, and his hands automatically cupped her hips and he smiled up at her. "Well, I like this."

Based on the bulge in his jeans, he certainly did. In response, she ground herself against him. The feeling thrilled her and they moaned in unison. Her mission was once again forgotten as he held her firmly in place while he drove his own clothed, wanting sex against hers. Using every bit of strength and control that she could muster, she grabbed his wrists, leaned over him and pushed at his arms until they were against the headboard above his head, resting on one of the slats.

Trevor laughed lustily and, while she held his wrists, he raised his head, so that his lips could just graze the tops of her breasts before she pulled away. "Not yet," she told him. She threaded the tie through the spaces on either side of the slat of wood closest to his head and then proceeded to tie an end to each of his wrists. Then she sat back so she could examine her handiwork and fully appreciate his prone form tied to the bed.

Trevor's body was impeccable, a testament to the time he spent at the gym and the muscles of his torso made even leaner from piloting his motorcycle every day. She admired the way his tattooed muscles and tendons tensed and flexed against his bindings.

He looked at her, lips pursed into a slight smile. "So, what now?" he murmured.

Abby had no freaking idea. She had this whole man to herself, but couldn't even decide how or where she wanted to start. She then looked Trevor up and down and decided that it didn't matter where she started first—she had all night. She could keep him there, take her time and explore his body. Even though they had slept together many times, he always took control and rarely gave her a chance to play with him. But tonight he was laid out in front of her and it was her turn. She wanted to know every inch of his skin, every muscle, every sensitive spot. She wanted to see if he was ticklish, where he like to be touched, what turned him on…

Well, she could see what turned him on. Based on the flare of his nostrils and the very prominent tent in his jeans, Abby knew that *she* turned him on. And she was certain she was about to blow his mind.

17

TREVOR TESTED THE strength of the knots Abby had used to bind his wrists. It was enough to hold him but not too tight. He knew that he could definitely pull himself loose if he wanted to. But there was no way in hell he was about to do anything to disturb her plans for the evening, so he just lay back and relaxed. Well, that wasn't exactly accurate. He was feeling a pretty long way from relaxed at that moment.

His eyes roamed over her body. She was amazing, and he wasn't exaggerating when he told her that she was the sexiest woman he'd ever seen. He yearned to touch her, to kiss her everywhere, before wrapping her legs tightly around his waist and plunging deep inside her. But he wouldn't, not yet. She'd gone to all of this trouble to get him where she wanted. And he wanted to see what she had planned for him. He'd play along, until it was his turn to take her, of course.

Whatever she had in mind, she'd better get on with it. With Abby in her current position, straddling his waist, he could feel her heat on his stomach. Then she leaned down, bringing her lips just millimeters from his own, just a breath of space between them. Her pink tongue darted out and traced the outline of his mouth. He raised his head again to kiss her properly, but she giggled and moved away. He was already painfully erect, and he rubbed against the fabric of his jeans. He gulped hard. Any more friction against his dick and he would come right then and there. Trevor sighed and threw his head back on the pillow. She wasn't going to make this easy for him and he had an inkling that, before long, he would be testing the tensile strength of the knots around his wrists.

"What's wrong, Trevor?" she purred, her lips whispering against his earlobe, a devilish smile alighting her red lips.

His patience and restraint had already worn thin. "Why don't you just untie me and we can have some fun together?" he breathed.

"I don't think so." She shook her head. "Plus, I'm kind of having *loads* of fun right now." She brought her mouth to his neck and kissed him.

"What's gotten into you?" he asked, shuddering when she dragged her teeth across his collarbone.

Abby returned to his ear and tongued the ridge of it, whispering in return, "Nothing's gotten into me." She reached down and grabbed his denim-clad member. She squeezed and a rough groan escaped his lips. "Not yet, anyway."

He shut his eyes and focused on the delicious agony that she was inflicting on his body. "You're trouble," he whispered. With every scrape of her fingernails across his skin, every lashing with her tongue, Trevor found himself getting closer and closer to insanity, and she had barely even touched him below the belt.

Abby traced the lines of his tattoos with her fingertips, while she licked and nibbled at his nipples and down his ribs to his navel. She was driving him wild. He tried to focus on something else, anything else, before he came. He couldn't remember ever being so near the edge, and, hell, he was still wearing his jeans.

"Jesus, Abby," he muttered.

She looked up at him, pausing her insanity-inducing ministrations. "What's wrong?"

"Just untie me."

"What's the magic word?"

Trevor sighed. He didn't want to beg. But if that's what it took…

"Abby, please." He closed his eyes.

Abby sat up. "I'm not going to untie you, but I'll give you what you want."

Trevor's eyes flashed open in time to see Abby move away from him. She stood briefly and grasped the barely there waistband of her miniscule thong and lowered it over her hips, letting it drop onto the floor. He took a deep breath and his mouth watered for her. He needed to taste her. It killed him that he couldn't get to her to do what he wished. And it was made all the worse when she reached behind her back and unclasped her bra, and her breasts were revealed. The only things that she was left wearing were her high heels, still buckled around her ankles, and the little jewel that adorned her belly button. It was almost too much to bear. She was perfect.

She reached over into his bedside table and pulled out the box of condoms that she knew was there from their previous encounters, and Trevor breathed a sigh of relief.

Finally!

Abby extracted one from the box, returned to the bed and took her place, once again straddling his thighs. In an extremely hot move, she closed her teeth around the wrapper, ripping the foil away with one clean jerk. She shifted back, kneeling at his knees, and she slowly, deliberately lowered his zipper. His cock sprang from the confined quarters of his jeans as she pulled them down over his hips and thighs and free of his feet. She paused a moment, looking him up and down.

Based on the way her chest heaved with every breath, he knew she was just as desperate for him as he was for her.

"When are you going to put us both out of our misery?" he asked, barely able to form words against the dryness in his throat.

"Soon…" she whispered, and she slowly, tortuously rolled the latex over him. He groaned, so close to breaking that he clenched his jaw and tried to concentrate on anything but how good her hands felt on him.

Once he was covered, Abby took him in her hand and held herself aloft for a moment. "Is this what you want, Trevor?"

"Yes," he murmured.

"I'm sorry, what did you say?" Abby played with him.

Trevor groaned as his restraint finally crumbled. He couldn't wait any longer. He pulled at his binding and one hand came loose. She squealed when his arms wrapped around her waist, and he rolled her over so that he was on top of her. She had deprived him of so much by not letting him feel her, taste her, that he was like a man starved of food and water. His hands and mouth touched her in any place they could.

He looked down, and his breath stopped at the sheer beauty she possessed. He wanted her. He wanted to hold her, protect her. Be with her forever—

He blinked, realizing that in bed, on top of Abby, wasn't exactly the time for introspection or analysis. And when he saw the raw passion etched on her face that definitely mirrored his own, he knew that he had to have her at that moment. He notched himself at her opening, and, with one forceful push, he plunged inside her.

He shuddered, completely surrounded, enrobed by her. Her mouth opened and he kissed her deeply. He withdrew and plunged back inside her. He didn't know if he would ever get used to the feeling of being inside her, and he didn't want to find out. It seemed every time he was with her, it was better than the last. He pulled her hips upward, at such an angle to allow him to get deeper.

"Oh!" she shouted.

Encouraged, he kept the angle but increased his speed and ferocity, hitting her in the same spot over and over until he felt her body tremble and stiffen and she clenched around his cock like a vise. She was coming and threatening to take him over the edge with her. He tried to hold back, to further her pleasure, but when her fingernails scraped across his shoulders, the piercing sensation did him in. Her thighs squeezed around his waist and she moved with him and they finished together, their breaths and cries mingled as he brought his lips back to her. He finally fully let go with a hoarse shout of his own. He exhaled a deep breath and rolled away from her, pulling her with him to his side.

It was a couple of minutes before he had the strength to push himself away from Abby. He wasn't quite sure what had happened to her tonight, what had gotten into her to act like that, to tie him up. Never in his life had he let himself be that vulnerable in bed with a woman. When it came to sex, he always called the shots but not with Abby. He'd actually *begged* her. That wasn't like him. But with Abby he didn't care.

LANGUIDLY, ABBY WALKED barefoot into Trevor's kitchen, wearing only the light blue button-down shirt that she'd found on his bedroom floor. It must have been a discarded work shirt, she reasoned; it smelled of his cologne mingled with his essence to create an intoxicating aroma that made her dizzy. She looked over her shoulder to make sure he wasn't behind her and she discreetly pulled the collar up to her nose and inhaled. She sighed at the pleasure the scent of him gave her.

"Are you actually wearing my old, funky shirt?" he asked with a laugh, coming up behind her. "Let me get you a clean one." He was still shirtless, but he had slipped into a pair of black pajama pants that lay low on his hips, exposing his defined abdominal muscles, hip bones and even the ghost of the rift of dark hair that disappeared behind the waistband.

"This is fine. I won't be wearing it for long."

"You're telling me," he said, waggling his eyebrows. He came up to her, put his hands on her hips and leaned in to kiss her.

"I mean that I'm not staying long," she said as she tried to push him away.

He frowned and reached past her to open the fridge. "There's no rush. You can stay as long as you like." He pulled out two bottles of beer and, with a flick of his wrist, he unscrewed the top of one and handed it to her.

She accepted it, suddenly parched. "Thanks."

"You hungry?" he asked.

Abby wasn't sure if it was the furious sex they'd just had or the fact that she hadn't eaten lunch that day, but she was ravenously hungry. She hadn't counted on staying at Trevor's after she was done torturing him, but, once she was in his apartment, she felt comfortable, like she was at home, and she wished that she didn't want to stay so badly. Before she could answer him, her stomach audibly growled.

"That sounds like a 'yes' to me." Trevor put down his beer and went back to the fridge. "Dinner it is! Unfortunately, I don't normally keep a whole lot of food here." She watched him pick through the vegetable crisper. She pursed her lips. For a guy who said he didn't keep a lot of food on hand, he sure had more fresh veggies in his fridge than she did. "I could pull together some spaghetti, or we could order in."

It had been so long since Abby had had time to cook anything outside a microwaved burrito or a bowl of cereal—like that was considered cooking. But her mouth watered at a homemade meal. "Spaghetti's fine."

"Sounds good. Just give me thirty minutes," he said, and busied himself, taking pots and pans from the cupboard. She watched him work shirtless as he chopped vegetables and made the red sauce from scratch. She had had no idea that he was skilled in the kitchen.

"Do you want a hand?"

He shook his head while he stirred his sauce, not looking away from it. He brought the wooden spoon to his lips, tasting as he went. "No, I've got it. You can go into the living room if you like. Watch some TV or something while I'm cooking."

Abby hated to drag herself away from him and the image he presented in front of the stove. Low-slung pants, just covering the curve of his ass. His back muscles tensing and flexing with every movement. There was nothing sexier than a man who knew his way around the kitchen. But she had to get away from him, if only for a moment. Her want for him was too strong, too powerful, that if she didn't leave the room, she might be forced to push everything to the floor and have him take her on the counter. Abby's stomach rumbled again as she realized that if she did that, they would never get dinner. So, she did the safe thing and turned on her heel and left the kitchen. She settled in front of the television. The large books on his coffee table caught her attention. She picked one up and then noticed another. Textbooks. She thumbed through the pages of one.

"What's with all of these textbooks?"

There was a beat of silence from the kitchen before she saw Trevor appear in the doorway. "Well, there's no sense in hiding it. I'm back in school."

Abby mouth dropped in both shock and glee. "What? That's great!" She looked at the cover of the book in her hand. "And you're taking finance?"

"Yeah, I'm studying business administration. I found a short course at the college to earn a diploma. I should be done in about six weeks. It's like a full course load, but it's really compressed into a shortened

amount of time. It's not really in-a
ing the basics of running a business.

"That's so fantastic. Why didn't you

Trevor shrugged. "I haven't really told ar
Jamie and now you." He disappeared back int...e
kitchen without another word, even though Abby still
had one hundred questions to ask him.

She gaped at the entrance to the kitchen, where
Trevor was cooking her a delicious-smelling dinner.
He was a good cook. And he was a student. Trevor was
full of surprises. She thought it weird that he hadn't
mentioned it. But she shrugged. *It's not like I'm his
girlfriend, or anything. It's his life.*

Abby reached past the pile of books for the remote
control, and a small scrap of paper fluttered to the
floor. Curious, she picked it up and studied it. It didn't
take a genius to figure out what it was. It was a phone
number. Above it was a name—Robin.

Robin's phone number. Who is Robin?

Abby smiled without mirth. She remembered the
woman riding on the back of his bike earlier that day.
Was that young, preppy girl Robin? She put the piece
of paper back in its rightful place. And she tried to
forget about it.

*Why should I care? I don't have any claim on the
guy.*

Abby turned on the television, trying to displace
her agitation. She settled for the news. Stories of inter-
national crises and despair, however, could not take
her attention away or stop her eyes from sliding to the
scrap of notepaper to her right. The swirling letters
and the perfectly formed numbers annoyed her, and
she was surprised that the *i* in Robin wasn't dotted

with a heart. She looked away and changed the channel to an entertainment news show. The bright lights, loud noises, flashing colors and whatever the host was rambling on about would surely distract her.

Who is Robin?

Why. Do. I. Care?

She was so intent on not worrying about whoever Robin was that she almost didn't notice when Trevor walked into the living room, holding two plates of steaming spaghetti. He handed one of them to her and settled in next to her on the couch.

"Thanks." Abby focused on the plate in front of her. "It smells delicious." She swirled some pasta around her fork and took a bite. Her eyes closed with pleasure as the flavors cascaded over her tongue. "Mmm…and it tastes delicious! This is incredible. Where did you learn to cook like this?"

TREVOR HESITATED. AT FIRST, he wasn't even sure that she had asked him a question. Just watching her enjoy the food he'd prepared with her eyes closed, head back and her delicate throat bobbing as she swallowed—the actions mimicking ones she made while in the throes of passion—was enough to make him hard again.

"My father taught me to cook some things," he said quietly, remembering the man who had raised him.

"He was a good cook?"

Trevor shrugged. "He always told me that a man should have at least one meal in his repertoire to impress women. So, he showed me a couple of things when I was younger."

"Not a bad lesson," she said, smiling. "What's he like?"

"My father?" he asked and she nodded. "He wasn't a bad man, but he had his vices—booze, women. He had one hell of a temper when he got going. It made my mom take off when I was a kid. Not that I can blame her. I left home when I was sixteen. My dad and I had a pretty bad fight, and then my brother and I went to live with my grandmother. Neither of us saw him much after that. And he died a few years back."

Abby was quiet. "I'm sorry."

"Don't be," he said with a shrug. "It was a long time ago. And I turned out just fine."

Neither of them said much as they ate. The television got Trevor's attention when Jamie's face flashed on the screen. The entertainment show's host was talking about a star-studded party that had just happened at Swerve Las Vegas. Jamie had texted him and told him it had gone well, and by the looks and the smiles on the faces of the A-list celebrities in attendance, Jamie and Swerve were well on their way to being the toast of Las Vegas. Trevor smiled at his best friend's success. Then his thoughts turned to his own life. His own bar was just sitting there, not open, not making him any money. He needed to get it up and running, and soon.

"How did you meet Jamie?" Abby broke the silence. She was also watching the television as they talked about Swerve.

Trevor told her about how they'd met at Shanahan's when they were teenagers.

She listened while she dug into her plate of pasta. "So, with exception of the courses that you're study-ing now, you never went to college?"

"No," he said quietly. It had always bothered him that he hadn't. But he didn't think much about it once he hit thirty. He figured the time for that had passed. But he was kind of proud that he'd finally gone back to school.

"How long have you wanted to go back?"

"Awhile." A change of subject was sorely needed. He had never felt so under a microscope as he did when she regarded him with her bright green eyes. Her scrutiny was too much for him. "What about you?" he asked her, finishing off his plate of pasta and putting it on the coffee table before them.

"What about me?" Abby also finished and followed suit.

"What's your story? Any sordid tales or debauchery in your history?"

"Well, I had a pretty typical upbringing..." She paused. "If you call a revolving door of men in and out of your mother's bedroom typical."

He frowned, and she smiled. "Don't be like that. I love my mom and she loves me so much. But she always makes me sad. She doesn't know how to be alone. It's impossible for her. She would meet one loser after another. Guys who were either unemployed or addicts or thieves. Losers and liars all of them. She falls in love in a day and then she thinks she can change them. But those types of guys, they won't change, they can't change. And she sacrificed so much of her life for them. She didn't get to realize her full potential because she was always taking care of some loser."

Trevor nodded, experiencing an aha moment. So that was it. That was where her commitment issues stemmed from. It was why Abby was so anti-relationship. It was why she couldn't trust him. He felt as if every day he was learning more and more about her. "That must have been hard for you as a kid."

She nodded. "It was. But look at me now!" She laughed.

"Well, aren't we just a couple of kids from broken homes?" He laughed with her. "Quite a wonder that we turned out as great as we did."

"It sure is."

The silence grew heavy and they were both aware of it, until Abby moved. He caught a glimpse of her soft thigh when the material of his shirt shifted with her, and he placed his hand on her. "I should go," she whispered.

Trevor frowned. He didn't want her to leave. "It's kind of late. Why don't you stay?"

She shook her head. "I can't."

"Why not?"

Her response was simple and emphatic. And he'd completely expected it. "Because I'm not my mother."

Trevor looked at her, confused. But that quickly made way for irritation. She was painting him with the same brush as all those losers that her mother had doted on. "What does your mother have to do with this?"

"I'm not looking for a relationship, Trevor. You know that." She stood away from his touch and looked down at him. "Especially with a guy like you."

"A guy like me?" He felt anger rising in his chest. "What does that even mean, *a guy like me?* Abby, I asked you to stay the night, not bear my children."

"You knew the rules when you agreed to this. If you want someone to spend the night, call one of your other girls."

Trevor was blindsided. He had no idea what she was

talking about. "There's nobody else, Abby. I'm not see-ing anyone but you."

"Sure." Her skeptical tone spoke volumes as she nodded, jutting her chin at the coffee table. He looked and saw the paper with Robin's number scrawled on it.

"Abby, no, listen—"

"I don't want to hear it," she snapped, refusing to listen to him. He knew then for sure that she didn't trust him.

She rolled her eyes and he was too hurt to look at her. If she didn't want to be with him, he wasn't going to force the issue. He picked up the remote control and switched the channel to a hockey game. "Maybe you should go," he told her, not taking his eyes from the television.

18

WHEN ABBY FINISHED work for the day, through some miracle, the sun was still in the sky. The past few days since she'd seen Trevor had been hard for her. She'd had trouble concentrating and she'd even made some more small—thankfully fixable—but frustrating mistakes. Not as bad as her *Poulin/Putain* error but just bad enough for her to still feel like an idiot. She could only blame her lack of concentration on the fight she'd had with Trevor. If she thought that the distractions that came with seeing him every day were bad, the alternative was so much worse.

She hated the way they'd left it, with her quietly getting dressed and walking out of his apartment. She had gone to him with a sexy revenge in mind, to make him forget about other women, but, at some point during the evening, her feelings had shifted. She and Trevor ate together and talked about their families. It was like they were a real couple, just hanging out after rocking each other's world in bed.

But when he'd denied being with that other woman, the one on his motorcycle, the one whose number he kept on the coffee table, it just showed that he'd lied to her, telling her that there was nobody else. It clearly wasn't the truth—she'd seen the woman with her own eyes. And that just proved her point that he would be no good for her.

And see what happens when you let him get under your skin even a little bit? she chided herself. *You're such an idiot, Abby. This is why you swore off men. Just forget him.*

Easier said than done, apparently. She thought of him almost every minute of the day. At work, at home, in bed. She pushed open the door to her office building and walked across the parking lot to her car. When she got close and looked up, she saw the motorcycle parked next to her car. The shiny chrome and metal gleamed in the setting sun. And there he stood. Trevor, leaning against his bike. Was he waiting for her?

She glowered. She was still mad at him, still hurt by his lie. And she wished she could remain indifferent to his presence, but she didn't think that was possible. "What are you doing here?"

He didn't answer her right away, so she unlocked her car and opened the door.

"I don't know why I'm here, really," he said. "I was driving by and I realized this is your office building. So I just stopped. I wanted to see you."

"How long have you been waiting here?"

He shrugged. "A little over an hour."

"It's a good thing that it's warm today."

"Yeah. It's downright balmy."

"Why are you here?" she asked, crossing her arms and leaning against her car.

Trevor blew out a breath. "It's been a couple of days.

I missed you. And I just wanted to apologize for the way we left things last time."

Abby didn't want to get into what had happened between them. She shook her head. "It's fine."

"I know what *fine* means. And it certainly doesn't feel *fine*. Intentionally or not, I feel like I might have crossed whatever your boundary is, and I'm sorry."

Abby nodded. It wasn't only that. But she let it go. "It's okay. After everything we've done in the past few weeks, asking me to stay the night shouldn't have elicited that kind of reaction."

"And I just want to explain about the phone number you saw. Robin's a girl in one of my classes. We study together. That's it." He looked at her. "But if this is just a casual thing—you and I—why did thinking that I was seeing someone else make you so angry?"

Abby had no response for that. He had a point. What could she say to him? There was no explanation.

"Why don't you hop on?" He smiled, patting the seat of the bike. "We'll go for a ride."

Abby scrunched her face in thought. Just minutes ago, she had told herself that she wouldn't see him again. Being with him would lead to nothing but trouble for her. But she forgot all of that when she saw him in his leather jacket, straddling the bike she'd liked so much.

"Come on," he said with a soft drawl that he must have known she wouldn't be able to resist. He withdrew another helmet from one of the saddle bags and handed it to her.

She took the helmet and strapped it under her chin. She put her work bag in the trunk of her car and slipped onto the back of the bike. She felt the cool steel between her thighs and it chilled her, but she was instantly warmed as his ass settled between her legs, and she fluttered involuntarily at him touching her most intimate flesh.

He turned and winked at her. He must have known that she would feel him there. He started the bike and the beast came alive with a roar under his command, and he pulled out of the parking lot.

Abby had never been on Trevor's motorcycle before, but other boyfriends had driven her on theirs. But those times felt like nothing compared to wrapping her arms around Trevor's waist and hitting the road. She felt free, and she loved it. And her breathing increased from the thrill of being on the back of his Harley.

No, wait!

She soon realized that her breathing wasn't accelerating from the thrill of the open road… It was actually the vibration from the motor and the tires gliding over the pavement that was revving her own engine. It went through her and her eyes widened. It was casual day at work, and she was wearing a pair of tight jeans, and the friction of the leather seating against her and Trevor's warmth between her legs made her breathing speed up and her cheeks flush. She could feel her nipples harden and a pool of moisture settle in her panties.

As if he knew what the bike was doing to her, Trevor sped up and took a turn. She turned into it with him and scooted closer, tightening her grip around his waist. With the increase in speed, the exhilaration and the desire built in her. She shifted against him, and clenched her thigh muscles together as much as she could while they remained spread, straddling the warm leather of the seat. It did nothing to dispel the desire she felt.

Trevor revved the engine higher and Abby thought she might pass out from the feeling. The scenery blurred around her and all she could focus on was the feeling between her legs and Trevor's leather-clad back in front of her. He revved the engine a few more times and Abby could feel her impending orgasm rising. It came over her in a wave and she rolled her head back, closing her eyes, as she came from the feeling of the engine under her and the air in her face.

The bike slowed and Abby's spasms subsided. She opened her eyes and looked around as Trevor pulled up next to her car. When he came to a complete stop, Abby regretfully tore herself away from him, wanting the ride and the feeling to last longer. She stood on shaky legs, removed her helmet and attempted to control her breathing before he could see how affected she was.

Too late. He removed his own helmet and flashed her a cocky, *knowing* smile. "Did you have a fun ride?"

Abby kept her smile neutral, not letting on how *fun* her ride actually had been. When she glanced down to his lap, in the light of the street lamp in the parking lot she could make out the shadow of the thick erection behind his own jeans. He wasn't so unaffected himself. "Yeah, it was a lot of fun. Thank you." She turned to open the door to her car.

"You look a little flushed. I hope I wasn't going too fast for you. Or maybe you're feeling a little under the weather?"

"I'm fine. Thanks, Trevor. Why don't you text me later?"

"I just might," he said.

"I'm free tomorrow night," she offered. "Do you have any plans?"

"Yeah, I do." He sighed. Abby felt a twinge of disappointment. "I'm coming over to your place," he said with a smile.

Abby laughed and leaned down to brush his lips with her own. She felt the same, familiar sizzle that came with every kiss. There was no denying it—she had missed being with Trevor. She couldn't wait to be with him tomorrow night.

She got into her car and shut the door. With a wave, she started the engine and pulled away. Through her rearview mirror, she saw that Trevor remained in the parking lot, watching her until she was safely on the road, before driving off in the opposite direction toward his own apartment.

19

ABBY HEARD THE knock on the door. She smiled and fluffed her hair and checked out her reflection in the mirror in her foyer. She knew it was Trevor. He had called a few minutes ago to say he was on his way over to see her. Since their fight a couple of weeks ago, and then the ride he'd given her on his motorcycle, Abby couldn't deny herself the pleasure that Trevor brought to her every time that they got together.

The knocking came again, and Abby made her way to the door and pulled it open. "That was quick—" Her smile fell when she saw the woman on the other side of the door.

Her mother was about Abby's height and shared her blond hair and green eyes, but years of bad habits and hard living had aged her significantly. It had been months since she had seen her.

"Mom?" Abby's mouth dropped. "What are you doing here?"

Her mother smiled and hugged her. "Abigail, don't look so happy to see me," she said, laughing, and walked into Abby's apartment.

"I'm just surprised. What are you doing here?"

"Does a mother need a reason to want to see her daughter?"

Abby recognized the hollow look in her mother's eyes, the exaggerated cheer in her voice that didn't mask the sadness. It was heartbreak. Another one of her mother's relationships had turned south, it would seem. It was a story that Abby had heard before.

"Mom…"

"Oh, it's nothing. Carl left. He just packed up and left. He cleaned out the bank account and everything."

"Oh, Mom." Abby hugged her mother. "I'm sorry."

So that's why she was there. The man in her mother's life had taken off, and now it was time for Abby to pick up the pieces. Until the next man came along, and then she was gone. Then the cycle would just repeat itself.

Abby's arms were wrapped around her mother's shoulders, as they had been many times before, whenever she had had a man run off or get caught cheating or end up in jail… Watching her mother go through this time and time again was the reason why Abby didn't trust men enough to be in a relationship, and why she didn't trust herself to be with Trevor. She didn't want to end up in her mother's shoes—haggard, tired, past her prime, alone.

"Oh, don't worry about me." Olivia waved a hand in front of her eyes and blinked them dry. "How's Luke?"

Abby was remorseful that she hadn't spoken to her mother in such a long time. But it wasn't like her mom had ever asked her about her life, her problems. "Mom, Luke and I broke up. Months ago."

"What?" Her mother was shocked. "Why? He was so good-looking. What happened?"

There were one thousand things that Abby would have rather done besides talk about Luke. "We wanted different things," she explained simply.

"What did he want?"

"He wanted a relationship. I wasn't ready for it, so I broke up with him."

"A relationship is a good thing," her mother told her.

Abby took in her mother's fragility. "Is it?"

"Yes, honey. It's good to have someone who loves you. Someone you can take care of. Someone to take care of you. So, are you seeing anybody else?"

Abby opened her mouth to speak, but she didn't get a chance as she was interrupted by a knock on the door. It was definitely Trevor. *Impeccable timing*. She closed her eyes, wishing that her mother or Trevor would just go away.

Abby's mother looked up. "Are you expecting anyone?"

"Yeah, but, Mom, I can reschedule."

"Oh, no, don't be silly. I should have called before I just came over here." Her mother stood and walked to the door. When she pulled it open and saw Trevor, she looked him up and down and turned to Abby with a sly smile. "Especially when you have this handsome young man coming over."

Typical, Abby thought, rolling her eyes. It seemed that all her mother needed to turn her mood around was to look at an attractive man.

Meanwhile, Abby wanted the earth to open up and swallow her. She did not need her mother to see her with Trevor. She could already imagine the constant barrage of questions that would be coming her way.

"Mom, this is my friend Trevor. Trevor, my mother, Olivia Shaw."

"Nice to meet you, ma'am." Trevor extended his hand.

Liv smiled broadly and turned to Abby. "Well, would you listen to this one, with his manners. Nice to meet you, doll," she said, shaking Trevor's hand and lingering a beat too long. "Abigail, I'll see you later."

Abby nodded and closed the door after her mother.

Trevor looked at Abby and smirked. "*Abigail?* Did I interrupt anything?"

"Nothing I'm not used to," Abby said before quickly giving Trevor the rundown of her conversation with her mother.

"Abby," Trevor whispered, pulling her into his arms, "I'm sorry."

"It's okay. I'm just tired of looking after her, you know?" Abby said into his shoulder. "She's the mother. She's supposed to be watching over me. Do you know what that's like?" Abby grimaced. "Oh, I'm sorry. I know your mother left. I can't believe I just said that."

"It's fine." He brushed his soothing palm over the back of her head, making her feel safe and cherished. She closed her eyes, relishing in the comfort he gave her. And she realized that it was nice to rely on someone else. "This isn't about me. I'm sorry she upset you."

"It's not like this is anything new. Same old story of Olivia Shaw." She snapped herself out of her trance and stepped back from the comfort of his warm arms. This was exactly what she didn't need—to become reliant on a man, only for him to walk out or screw her over.

"Forget that." She took a few steps back, just to make sure she was safely at a distance. "You know what? We're both here now. Let's just forget all that happened and get on with our evening," Abby said. Reaching up and wrapping her arms around Trevor's neck, she forcefully drew his mouth down to hers and kissed him deeply.

She led Trevor into her bedroom, where she could forget about her mother's problems. But she couldn't totally forget about the sadness in her mother's eyes. The hurt that all of the men, the losers, inflicted upon her. Abby had to look after herself, to protect her heart. She wouldn't let herself get hurt. But that didn't mean that she couldn't have a little fun with Trevor at the same time.

20

TREVOR TURNED ON the water and tested the temperature on his hand. Abby stroked his back, and his muscles twitched under her fingers, as they did every time she touched him.

"What's taking so long?" she asked, standing behind him, her hands sailing down his ass and squeezing hard.

"I'm making sure it isn't too hot."

"You should know by now that I like it hot, Trevor," she said as she reached around to his front and stroked him.

Trevor laughed through his groan and turned to her. He put his hands on her waist and, without much of a struggle, he lifted her into the shower stall.

She squealed. "Trevor, that's cold."

"Sorry." He followed her inside and stood under the showerhead, shielding her from the spray until the temperature regulated. The sharp needles of cold water hit his back, cooling the hot trails that her fingers had drawn on his skin. It soothed him. "You should have been more patient."

After Abby's mother had left, Abby had wasted no

time dragging him into her bedroom, where they had a quick, frenzied union. Abby had been on fire and she took everything she'd needed from him. After they'd regained their breath, Abby announced that she needed a shower and asked him to join her.

He was surprised by her invitation, as she had stated before that showering together was too intimate. But he wasn't about to say no. *Like I would ever pass up that opportunity!*

The water now warm, Abby stood underneath the spray and raised her arms to rinse her hair. He watched, transfixed, as the water cascaded over her breasts and down her stomach.

"You're so beautiful, Abby," he whispered. He wasn't even sure that she had heard him, until she took a step toward him in the narrow stall, so that they were chest to chest.

"You're not so bad yourself."

He leaned in and kissed her, and her arms snaked over his shoulders and her wrists linked at his neck. Losing control, he pushed her lightly against the wall and pressed into her. His hands found her breasts. They fit perfectly in his palms and he cupped them, pinching her nipples between his fingers.

Trevor found himself once again rock hard. With Abby, he always had the stamina. He needed no reprieve to regain his strength. He never stopped needing Abby. His cock stood straight up and it was pressed between them, sliding with the slickness of the water on their bellies. He needed her again. And soon. But, dammit, he realized that neither of them had brought a condom into the bathroom. But he forgot all reason when she slid up and down his front, torturing his swollen cock between them.

Trevor groaned and held her up against the wall of her shower. The water beaded against his back and it kept her reasonable dry as he pinned her in place. He lifted her and her legs wrapped around his waist.

ABBY NEEDED THE blessed release that she knew he would provide. "Trevor, I want you," she whispered. She had misspoken, of course; it wasn't just that she wanted him. She needed him. She needed to feel him everywhere. His mouth was on her shoulder; he was driving her wild with his lips, tongue and the light nibbles from his teeth. She sighed. "Now."

Trevor paused and pulled away and looked in her eyes. His hair fell in his face, beads of water rolling over him. "Are you sure?" he asked.

"It's fine. I'm on the pill," she breathed. "Let's just do it."

"Are you sure?" he asked again.

"I'm sure."

"Abby—"

"I trust you. Just do it already. I need you."

He kissed her and spread his stance, grounding himself, gaining purchase on the rubber adhesives on the floor. He primed himself at her entrance and pushed inside her. He grunted in her ear, and she threw back her head. The sound of their sighs reverberated in the shower, bouncing off the ceramic tiles, surrounding her.

Her desire rose in waves, starting at her center, rushing throughout her body as he thrust his hips back and forth, angling her just so that his shaft was at the right angle to rub against her clit, the sensitive bud of nerves alighting and bringing her to an orgasm that crested and crashed over her. She came, she squeezed him and she felt him stiffen and he stroked, emptying himself inside her.

"Christ," he murmured quietly, tonguing the sensitive skin of her neck. "Abby, I love you."

Her eyes flew open. Did she hear that right? He dropped her gently to stand on her feet. He opened the shower door and reached for her towel. Wordlessly, he ran the soft cotton over her, drying her. When he finished, she mumbled a quick thank-you and headed for her bedroom.

ABBY SIGHED AND stared at the ceiling. Trevor was still in the bathroom. She replayed his words over in her head. Three simple words, small words, each of them, but filled with the largest of meaning.

Abby, I love you.

He loved her. It wasn't supposed to happen like that. He wasn't supposed to fall in love with her. She frowned. This wasn't supposed to be a relationship. It was against the rules.

But if it was against the rules, why did his admission fill her with equal parts happiness and fear? Confused tears formed in her eyes and she tried her hardest to blink them away. No use. One escaped, trailing over her cheek, and she quickly wicked it away. She had no idea what to make of how she felt. Did she love him, too? She shook her head stubbornly, admonishing herself. She wasn't allowed to fall in love with him.

She heard the toilet flush. She had no idea what to say to him.

"Abby." She heard his voice come from the doorway. He sounded as hesitant as she felt. Maybe he regretted saying the words; maybe they slipped out in a moment of blind passion and he didn't mean them and he wasn't sure how to take them back? But thinking about him rescinding his admission of love caused new tears to form in her eyes. *God, I'm a mess.*

He came to her on the bed and sat beside her. "Listen…"

"You don't have to apologize." She sat up, clutching the bedsheet to her chest. "You said something that you didn't mean to. The words just slipped out."

Trevor shook his head. "No, that's not it. Abby," he said quietly, "I feel like I need to finally talk to you about this. I know that you don't want a relationship, but if you don't let me tell you how I feel, I might explode."

"Trevor, don't—" She tried to stop him before he said it again. She couldn't hear it again. She was afraid she might fall apart if she did.

"Abby, I love you. And I've been in love with you for a long time."

"You have to stop. That's not allowed," she stammered, trying to regain her composure, her resolve. She couldn't look at him.

"According to who?"

"Me. I'm not—"

"Looking for a relationship," he finished for her, having heard it before. "I know. Goddammit, don't I know it." He stopped and looked at her—no, *through her.* Realization lit his eyes. "This is about your mother, isn't it? About why she was here?"

She glared at him. *How dare he?* She had no response. But she looked at the floor, the ceiling, until her gaze finally landed back at him. "Why are you doing this?" she whispered.

"*Why am I doing this?* What, confessing my love to you? Putting myself on the line, telling you how I feel? Abby, whether you like it or not, there's more to this," he said, waving a hand between them. "There's more to you and me. Tell me there isn't."

She hesitated, even though she knew that there was something far greater than lust happening between herself and Trevor. But she still couldn't bring herself to say the words.

He exhaled a frustrated breath. "You're not your mother. You just told me that you trusted me. Was that a lie? Don't you trust me not to hurt you?" When she said nothing, he took a deep breath and looked around the room. "You know, I don't like being used, Abby," he said quietly, reaching for his pants, which were rumpled on the floor. He pulled them up while he looked around for his shirt.

She stood, throwing the bedsheet aside. She was naked so she reached for her robe. She tied the belt around her waist. "Who's using you, Trevor? You're getting just as much out of this as I am."

He found his shirt and began to button it up. He stopped when his shirt was only half buttoned. He stared at her. "No, I'm not. I need all of you, Abby, or none of you. And if there's nothing more to this than sex, it has to end. I can't do this anymore."

Abby nodded. His words were like a punch to her chest. She turned her back to him as he walked out of the room. She wanted nothing more than to call out to him, tell him to come back, but she wouldn't. She couldn't bring herself to do it. It was better that way. They needed to end it. They should have ended it before they both got in too deep.

With the slam of the door, Trevor was gone. She curled up in a ball on her bed, unable to staunch the flow of tears.

TREVOR WALKED ACROSS the parking lot to his car. The night air was warm but he still felt the chill from Abby. He pulled open the driver's side door and dropped onto the seat. He slammed the heel of his hand against the steering wheel. He'd been an idiot. He knew that Abby wasn't ready to hear anything close to a declaration of love. And the worst of it was that, while he was definitely in love with her, he hadn't even meant to say it.

But it was just the feeling, the way she felt wrapped around him, unencumbered by a layer of latex, her breath in his ear, the warm water pelting his back. Being with Abby was more incredible than anything he'd ever felt, and he had royally screwed it up.

His phone buzzed in his pocket. He picked it up, thinking that it might be Abby, hoping it was, but when he illuminated the screen, he saw that it was a text from Jamie.

Coming to town tomorrow. I scored some awesome suite tickets for the Raptors game in Toronto. Playoffs, baby! Want to come with?

He didn't really want to go anywhere, especially out of town. But maybe some time out at a basketball game with Jamie would make him feel better, take his mind off what had just happened between him and Abby.

What about Maya?

She doesn't want to go. Be my date?

Sure, but I'm not putting out.

Well, forget it then. Invitation rescinded.

Trevor laughed. Since he'd known the guy, they'd always been able to cheer each other up.

Sure, I'll go.

Great. See you then.

Trevor started the engine and took one last look at the window that he knew was Abby's apartment. He watched the light she'd left on in the living room turn dark. He wished that he'd played it differently. That he hadn't told her how he felt. He'd known better. He should have just kept his mouth shut.

Trevor backed out of his parking space and pulled out on to the road. He thought of all of the things going on in his life at the moment. All of the things that he had to juggle—opening the bar, studying for his final exams. He was at the beginning of a new life and it was important to focus on that. Maybe ending things with Abby was for the best.

ABBY TOOK A breath and closed the slide-show presentation that she had just given to François and all of the bigwigs of Ashbourne Cosmetics. She had come up with an exceptional marketing plan, if she did say so herself, and all of the smiling faces around the table seemed to agree. Despite Abby's faux pas in their early correspondence, Sylvie Poulin also smiled at her, pleased with everything Abby had laid out.

"Does anybody have any questions?" Abby fielded the typical questions and then a few that she hadn't prepared for, but she still handled them like a pro.

"Abby, I think that you have an excellent plan here and we can move forward with this immediately."

Abby smiled and, on the exterior, she kept her cool, all the while doing a booty-shaking happy dance on the inside. She shook the hand of each person as she gathered her things and they all filed out of the room. Behind them, Abby was elated as she headed for her desk.

She wanted nothing more than to pick up her cell phone, dial Trevor's number and share the good news with him. But she highly doubted that he would want anything to do with her after the way she'd treated him.

Her cell phone buzzed next to her arm. She closed her eyes, imagining that it was from Trevor. He had called and texted her several times, apologizing. He felt bad. And so did she. But she couldn't bear to think about him—she couldn't, what with the figurative, giant, gaping hole in her chest. She picked up her phone and was both disappointed and relieved to see that it was a text from Maya, letting Abby know that she would be in town later that night. Jamie had meetings scheduled for the next few days and Maya was tagging along.

Boarding right now. Love you, girl. Can't wait to see you.

Have a safe flight. See you soon, Abby responded.

Abby was relieved that Maya would be in the city in a matter of hours. That's what she needed. A little time with her best girlfriend to take her mind off all things Trevor.

21

"WHAT'S GOING ON WITH YOU?" Maya asked Abby, as she listlessly stirred her coffee. "The small amount of sugar that you put in there has long since dissolved by now."

Abby stopped stirring and looked into her cup. "You're probably right." She shrugged and took a sip. "There is nothing going on with me," Abby muttered. "I'm fine." Even though she was grateful for her best friend's company, Abby had no intention of discussing what had happened with her and Trevor the night before.

Upon landing, Maya had come immediately to Abby's apartment. Seeing what a wreck she was, Maya had urged Abby to go out. She'd suggested going for dinner, cocktails, a movie, shopping and roller-skating, just to name a few activities—anything she could think of to stop Abby from moping. But Abby didn't want to do anything but drink coffee in her apartment. Her fight with Trevor was still fresh in her mind and whenever she thought about it, it felt like her heart was being ripped violently from her chest.

Maya straightened and folded her arms across her

chest. She said nothing and Abby felt her friend's scrutiny. "I know what's going on here," she concluded.

"And what's that?"

"Let's go over the scene, shall we? Your apartment's a mess, you're not wearing makeup, your hair's a disaster, you're in your sad-girl sweats." Maya stood and opened the fridge and scanned the inside. "And—*aha!*—nothing in the fridge but chocolate, Thai takeout and white wine." Maya retrieved the wine and closed the door, before turning back to Abby. "I know what this is. You, Abby Shaw, are going through relationship problems. And you even got some great career news and yet we aren't out celebrating because you're moping."

Dammit. Maya was good. Abby should have known that she couldn't escape the watchful eye of her best friend. "I am not," she said. "And I am excited about work." But why wasn't she happy, even after she had everything that she thought she wanted in her career? "Plus, I would have to be in a relationship to have any problems associated with said relationship."

"Does this have anything to do with Trevor?"

Abby looked squarely at her friend. "I'm afraid I have no idea what you're talking about."

"Seeing as how you haven't told me about any other guys in your life at the moment, I can only assume your current emotional state is because of Trevor Jones, the man you're currently sleeping with. The one you are *not in a relationship* with."

Abby shook her head. "That's neither here nor there. And we aren't sleeping together. Not anymore."

Maya sat back on her stool at the breakfast bar, her face marked with concern. "What happened?"

"It is about Trevor," Abby conceded with a sigh. Maya was silent, and Abby continued, telling her about the fight they'd had. How Trevor had told her that he loved her and her less-than-gracious response. When she finished, she looked at Maya. "You can say it now. *I told you so*."

Maya shook her head, reached across the table and covered Abby's hand with her own. "I won't say that. Ever. Especially because you're hurting. But I have a question. Why did you start sleeping with him?"

Abby shrugged. "Look at him. I wanted him. He's just so sexy."

"And he fell in love with you."

Abby nodded. "I knew his reputation and I thought I could rely on the fact that he would just want to keep it casual, not want to settle down, and that's what I wanted, too. But then, when he started saying all of these beautiful things to me, I just couldn't deal with it. And I'm so screwed up that I couldn't trust him, even though he'd given me no reason not to. I was so awful to him and then I kicked him out."

TREVOR WATCHED THE action on the court, and even though the Raptors were his favorite basketball team, and they'd recently clinched a spot in the playoffs, he was barely paying attention to the game. He even remained seated when Jamie stood and pumped his fist.

"Yeah!" Jamie cheered. He sat back down and saw that Trevor hadn't reacted to the basket. He elbowed Trevor. "What's up with you, man?"

"Huh?" Trevor barely heard him. He drank from his beer, distracted. Apparently he hadn't been paying attention to Jamie, let alone the basketball game.

"Aren't you watching this?" Jamie gestured to the court. "That was a beautiful shot."

"Oh, yeah," Jamie muttered. He didn't want to admit that he hadn't even seen the shot in question. When Trevor looked back to Jamie, his friend was scrutinizing him. "What?"

Jamie swiveled the leather chair in which he was sitting to face Trevor. "What's wrong with you?"

They were enjoying all of the privileges and the perks of being in an executive box suite at the Air Canada Centre, which they were sharing with several other men, who considered networking and being seen in an expensive suite more important than the game itself. Businessmen who tried to approach Jamie but walked away, sullen, when he showed no interest in anything other than the action on the court.

"Nothing's wrong." Jamie wasn't looking away. "I'm just tired. School, the club, getting the new place ready. It's exhausting."

"Yeah, I'll bet," Jamie agreed. "You're sure there's nothing else going on?"

"What could be going on?"

"Oh, I don't know. Maybe you're having some sort of female trouble. Problems with Abby, maybe?"

Trevor turned in his own chair and stared at his friend. "I don't think so." He took another swallow from his beer, draining it, and then went to the fridge in the bar area and retrieved two more bottles for himself and Jamie. He twisted the tops off both and handed one to Jamie. "Nothing's wrong," he repeated, sitting back down.

Jamie was clearly unconvinced. "Well, if that's the case and you aren't all torn up for some reason about

Abby, I've got the *sexiest* woman to introduce you to. She lives in Vegas, so it can just be a casual hookup thing."

Trevor grimaced at his friend's phrasing.

"She works with Maya," he continued. "Gorgeous woman, funny, too, perfect figure, legs for days..."

Trevor didn't even look at Jamie. He didn't care about some random woman at Maya's office. He wasn't interested in meeting anyone. He was in love with Abby. "Not interested," he muttered, staring back at the court.

"Okay, now I know it's a female problem. You have *never* passed up a gorgeous woman that I wanted to introduce you to." Jamie laughed.

Trevor rolled his eyes. "What are you talking about?"

"I'm fucking with you. There's no one I want you to meet in Vegas. At least not until you tell me what happened. I know it's about Abby because you would have definitely told me if you were seeing anyone else."

Trevor sighed in resignation. "You got me."

"So, what's up?"

Trevor took a pull from his beer and cast a look back at the other occupants of the box. He wasn't interested in talking about it, especially within earshot of other people. But they were all oblivious to anything other than their own stories and smug laughter. "I fell in love with her."

"What?"

Trevor shrugged. "I love her."

"You, Trevor Jones, are in love and pining for a woman? What happened to just hooking up?"

Trevor caught the pitying gaze that his friend shot at him. He sighed. He didn't want Jamie's pity.

"But I don't understand. If you're in love with her, isn't that a good thing?" Jamie asked him. "Why are you so miserable?"

"So, WHY ARE you so miserable?" Maya asked Abby.

"I don't know. I miss him—" Abby buried her face in her hands.

"But you don't want to be with him," Maya supplied.

"Yes. No. I don't know." *Do I want to be with him?* She had no real idea. Even talking it out made her more confused.

"Are you in love with him?"

"No," she answered immediately but without conviction.

"Are you sure?"

Abby said nothing. She wasn't sure about anything. "I don't know. I don't want to be in love."

"Sometimes it's not your choice. I don't think we get to choose who we fall in love with. Don't you think that my life would have been a lot easier if I hadn't completely fallen for my boss?" Maya alluded to being hired by Jamie and then becoming his lover. "All of the heartache we both went through? We could have avoided that by choosing not to be in love. But we couldn't. It wasn't up to us. We are all powerless against love. Maybe his admission made you realize that you have feelings for him. Maybe that's why you freaked out."

Abby opened her mouth to speak. But she said nothing. Did she *love* Trevor? She was fond of him and loved him as a friend. But when she thought of him, a hollow opened in her chest and she found it difficult to breathe. This is exactly what she hadn't wanted—to fall in love and not be in control. She didn't want to feel like this over some guy. But Trevor wasn't just *some guy*.

"How did you know that you were in love with Jamie?" Abby asked her friend.

"This *is* serious." Maya went to the freezer and pulled out a carton of double-chocolate cookie-dough ice cream. "The good stuff," she noted. "You really are depressed," she muttered, grabbing two spoons from the cutlery drawer. When she sat back down across from Abby, they both dug into the ice cream.

"You actually made me realize that I was. You told me that the surest sign that I was in love with Jamie was that I wasn't able to live without him. When not being with him *hurt*. I knew that I was in love with Jamie when all I could think about was the next time I would see him. When I was so miserable without him that I knew I wouldn't be happy until I saw him again."

Abby nodded, numbly. She could imagine that. She felt like she was falling apart, and she wouldn't feel whole again until Trevor put all of her pieces back together.

"I TOLD HER that I was in love with her and she completely freaked out," Trevor explained.

"What do you mean, she freaked out?"

"Exactly that. I knew better. I knew that she didn't want to get any feelings involved and I didn't mean to say it. But when I tried to explain to her how I feel, Abby wouldn't hear it and she kicked me out of her apartment."

Jamie nodded, absorbing the words Trevor had told him. "Well, does she love you back?"

"If she does," Trevor said, laughing without humor, "she's got one hell of a way of showing it."

"She set the rules for the arrangement, right?" Jamie asked. "Are you so obtuse that you never considered that she's afraid? Commitment-phobic, maybe? Trust issues?"

Trevor exhaled. Abby fit into all of the above categories. "Well, look at you, Mr. Relationship Advice—"

"I thought it wasn't a relationship," Jamie countered with a straight face and a knowing stare.

Jamie rolled his eyes at Trevor and took a long drink from his bottle. "She definitely is commitment-phobic," Trevor explained. "There's more at play, though. She's got some issues that go back to her mother. But, whatever it is, it doesn't matter. It's too late now. It's over. I tried calling and texting, but she won't even respond. She won't talk to me. But more than anything, I miss being her friend."

"Well, I hope you guys are willing to put it behind you for an evening," Jamie said. "Because Maya wants us all to go out to dinner tomorrow before we head back to Vegas."

Trevor opened his mouth and shook his head. "What? No, I can't," he stated emphatically.

"You have to," Jamie told him. "It's what Maya wants, and Maya gets what she wants."

"I THINK I'M in love with Trevor," Abby said quietly, staring into the ice cream.

Maya smiled. "I'm glad to hear you admit it. But why are you so upset about it? He's a good guy, and it sounds like he really loves you, too. But, honey, why are you talking to me? Why don't you tell him?"

She shook her head. "I can't. It's too late. I wouldn't even know what to say. The way I treated him…" she trailed off sadly. "Even if I told him that I feel the same way, there's no way he would even take me back. I'm scared."

"Love is scary."

"How am I supposed to just give this huge chunk of myself to one person?"

"Here's the thing, Abby. When you're in love with someone and you give them that *huge chunk* of yourself, they go ahead and give you one right back."

Abby gaped at Maya. "How did you get so smart about this?"

"Lots of embarrassing, painful experience," Maya said, laughing.

"What am I going to do?" Abby sighed and leaned back on her stool.

"Well, I guess you've got a little bit of time to figure it out. You're meeting me and Jamie for dinner tomorrow night. Trevor's going, too."

"What?" Abby froze. She couldn't face Trevor. "No, I don't think so." This was exactly what she was afraid of—that she and Trevor would never be able to be face-to-face again.

"Are you kidding me? We're going back to Vegas the next evening, and I won't be back for a few months. I need to see you. And I need my best friend to be able to be in the same room with my future-husband's best friend," Maya pleaded. "Do it for me."

The last thing Abby needed was to see Trevor, but, for Maya, she would do anything. "Sure. I'll be there."

22

THE RESTAURANT THAT Jamie and Maya had chosen was one of the best in the city and they had an excellent table that afforded them a great deal of privacy. Abby took a sip from her wineglass. She tried to distract herself by discussing wedding plans with Maya. But it didn't work—the constant awareness of Trevor beside her was almost too much to bear. Every time he shifted in his seat or his cologne drifted past her nose, it grabbed her attention, as did the rich baritone of his voice when he spoke to Jamie. But she never turned to look at him. She sat rigidly in her chair. She couldn't risk turning to address him. She took another sip of wine. Self-medicating with alcohol, in hopes of dulling her senses around him, seemed to be the best way for her to survive the evening.

At least when she and Trevor were friends, they were able to carry on a simple, civil conversation. Her heart ached for the time they'd spent together. Abby knew that she had ruined everything with her suggestion they be friends with benefits and then with stupid resistance to a real relationship with Trevor, no matter how perfect he was for her.

Maya was saying something about color schemes, and she tried her hardest to pay attention, but she wasn't able to think clearly until Trevor excused himself to go to the restroom. Abby, Jamie and Maya watched him leave.

Maya leaned in to her and spoke quietly. "Have you talked to him yet?"

"No," she said, reaching for her wineglass.

Jamie cleared his throat. "So, I'm to assume that this very awkward and uncomfortable dinner is all because of what happened between you two?" He raised his eyebrows. "You guys sleeping together, him telling you he loves you and you completely losing it at him?"

Maya joined Abby in glaring at him. "Jamie," Maya hissed at him. "How did you know about that?"

Jamie raised both palms. "He's my best friend. There are some rare moments when we tell each other things." And he pointed his finger at Abby. "And you've got him tied up into such knots that he can barely even think straight."

"Jamie," Maya admonished him again.

"I'm allowed to defend my friend," Jamie said, before taking a mouthful of wine and draining his glass, while Maya glared at him.

"It's okay," Abby insisted. And now Maya and Jamie were fighting because of her. It seemed that she had a disastrous effect on everyone's relationships. "I had that coming."

"You sure do," Jamie continued, and Abby knew the moment that Maya's high heel spiked into his foot. "Ouch!" He turned back to Abby. "For what it's worth, though, I think you should cut him a little slack. He's definitely just stressed out about school and the new bar." He speared a piece of lettuce from his salad and put it in his mouth.

"The new bar? What are you talking about? I knew he was in school, but—"

Jamie's mouth fell open. "He didn't tell you?"

Abby shook her head. "Tell me what? What's going on?"

"I'm such an idiot. I probably shouldn't have said anything. He's been keeping it under wraps. He bought a bar. This pub where we used to work. I don't know how he actually had any time to see you with everything he's had on his plate lately."

Abby couldn't believe that he had kept that from her. But before she could ask any questions, Jamie stood.

"Maya, let's dance."

"Jamie, this is a restaurant. We can't dance here," she protested with a laugh.

"There's music. There's a spot by the bar. We can dance."

"But we can't leave Abby."

"Don't worry about me. Go, dance, have fun," she told them.

Trevor still hadn't returned. He was surely avoiding her, so Abby sat alone and watched Jamie and Maya as they danced to the soft jazz the pianist was playing. She smiled. They were the only people dancing and if they realized it, they didn't care. They spoke softly to each other and laughed, as Jamie swirled her around the makeshift dance floor. Jamie and Maya were so completely in love with each other.

Abby felt her eyes glaze over with a wistful sheen,

quickly catching the tear that made its escape. Maya and Jamie were amazing together. She had never seen her friend so happy and carefree before. Jamie's hands encircled Maya's waist, holding her close to him, and it hit Abby. That's what she wanted.

She wanted a man to look at her like she was the only woman in the world. She wanted the comfort, peace and security that could only come from the right man's arms—how she'd felt in Trevor's arms. Who was she kidding? She did love him and she wanted to be with him. But she couldn't tell him. She had already so brutally pushed him away, and he couldn't even stand to be in the same room with her. It was all too much for her. She had to get the hell out of there.

She took one final look at Maya and Jamie, and then she pulled a pen and a scrap of paper from her purse and scrawled out a note of apology to them and left it on the table. She picked up her scarf from the back of her chair, wrapped it over her shoulders and found the nearest exit.

TREVOR HAD SEEN her note and found her almost immediately. He sighed when he saw her standing at the edge of the parking lot. Her arms were crossed over her chest and her chin held a strong, defiant upward tilt. He walked up to her. "Abby, come back inside."

"How did you know I was out here?" she asked without looking at him.

"I saw your note, that you weren't feeling well. I didn't know if you were still out here or not. But I was hoping that you hadn't left yet." He reached out and put a hand on her arm. "Come back inside."

"No, my cab should be here soon." She looked up the street, as if she could see it.

"Why did you leave?"

"You read my note. I'm not feeling well."

"It's funny. I'm not feeling well, either. And I haven't been since the day I left your apartment."

Abby said nothing, but Trevor could see her slight shiver as the cool air of the night hit her bare legs and every other piece of skin not covered by her over-size scarf. When would the woman ever buy an actual jacket?

She was quiet and then looked down at her feet. "I'm sorry we're not friends anymore," she said with a frown.

"We aren't?"

"No. I ruined everything by suggesting we start sleeping together. By telling you that you couldn't love me." She paused and looked up at him. He wanted to kiss away the sadness he saw on her face. "If we were friends, you would have told me about your bar."

He opened his mouth. "How—" And then he realized. "Jamie told you?"

"Yeah. He also gave me a piece of his mind."

"What?" Trevor was upset that his friend would interfere. "Son of a bitch. That guy has the biggest mouth." He put a hand on her shoulder, his fingers instinctively curling around the soft skin and the curve of her clavicle. Her skin was slightly chilled. "Abby, you're cold." He shrugged out of his jacket, placing it over her. He pulled the lapels together to provide her with some warmth.

"I'm fine," she maintained. "I don't get cold."

"What if I knew how to warm you up?" he said, winking.

She smiled briefly. The fleeting upturn of her lips was replaced by a frown. Trevor took in the sadness that was on her face. The sadness that had been on her face the entire night.

"I'm sorry that I didn't tell you about the bar. I didn't really tell anyone. I should have been honest."

Abby sniffed. He noticed the thin sheen of moisture in her eyes that threatened to spill. He stepped closer to her. "What's wrong?"

Tears formed in her eyes. "Nothing."

"Abigail..." he chided her with a small smile.

She looked away and blinked, causing a tear to fall down her cheek. He raised his hand and caught the moisture on his thumb. He swiped the tear away, but his palm remained, arching over her cheek.

Trevor's heart thundered in his chest. No matter how much he tried to ignore it, put it away to save himself the heartache of her unrequited love, he loved Abby more than anything. He looked into her eyes. They glistened. He dropped his mouth to hers and kissed her.

With that one kiss, he was lost. His hand slid around to the back of her head and he pulled her to him. He heard her soft sigh and she opened her mouth under his, allowing him to deepen the kiss. His tongue found hers and he held her tighter, wishing the kiss would never end.

ABBY RELUCTANTLY PULLED away from him. "Trevor..."

"Yeah?"

She hesitated and took a deep breath and a chance. "Is it too late for us?"

"Too late?" he asked her. "Do you want to start hooking up again? I don't think that's a good idea—"

"No," she interrupted him, taking an almost imperceptible step back. "Do you think it's possible for us to start over? Do you think we could be together? Like, in a relationship? I'm sorry I hurt you, and I'm miserable without you. But I was so focused on my own life, and my own problems, that I never once considered your feelings."

Trevor's eyes widened. "Abby, it's okay. You were right in what you said. I had as much fun when we got together as you did."

"Trevor, stop talking." She brought her fingertip to his lips. "What I'm saying is this—I'm in love with you."

She heard his quick intake of breath, and when he didn't respond, she searched his face for some sign of what he was thinking. She didn't remember ever being so nervous. He had every right to laugh in her face and walk away, tell her to get the hell out of his life.

But finally he smiled. "Get over here."

Abby went to him with no hesitation. She exhaled her relief. When he had gone what felt like an hour without saying anything, she thought she was about to go crazy. His arms encircled her waist and it felt like she was home. He leaned in and kissed her. How she could deny herself the pleasure of his love, she had no idea. "I'm sorry I couldn't see it before. I love you," she repeated. Once she'd said those words, she knew that she would never be able to stop.

"I love you, too, Abby," he whispered, before leaning in to kiss her again.

23

TREVOR LOOKED AROUND the bar. The music was loud, but he barely heard it over the laughs and the jocular conversation of everyone around him. The sound of people enjoying themselves was nearly deafening. It was a good sign. People were having fun. Silence would have been a death knell. Langered, its name a throwback to his Irish roots, was nearly filled to capacity with friends, well-wishers, reviewers and industry insiders. Jamie and Maya were talking to old friends and Robin, his new assistant manager, and some of her friends had taken up a table in a quieter corner. The only face missing was the one he longed to see the most—Abby's. She had texted him to say that she'd had a busy day at work and that she was running late, but she was on her way.

He dipped his forefinger underneath the too-tight collar of his shirt and tie and pulled, trying to loosen the constricting material. He was the owner of Langered Pub and, even though he hated wearing a suit, he figured that he might as well try to look *respectable* on his opening night. He checked his watch—only a couple of more hours and he could lock up the doors and take off the godforsaken tie.

He took another glance around the bar, surveying for any trouble, mistakes or something he might have overlooked. Searching for a problem, for something to go wrong. But nothing was wrong, everything was perfect and he didn't trust it. He was still tense. And he could think of only one way to relieve the tension... but Abby wasn't anywhere in the building.

Trevor jumped slightly when he felt a hand drop on his shoulder. When he turned, he saw that it was Jamie.

"How are you holding up?" Jamie asked. "Seems like you can't even breathe over here."

"Breathing is a little tough right now," Trevor admitted, pulling once again at his shirt collar. "I don't know how you do this, opening new clubs and hotels all the time. I just keep waiting for something to go wrong."

Jamie shook his head. "It's always stressful. But I don't think you have to worry. This is one hell of a party." Jamie looked around the club. "Everything looks great. People are having a good time. You've covered all of your bases."

Jamie rubbed the back of his neck. And Trevor knew that was one of Jamie's tells, that his friend was feeling some strain. "Can we go into your office for a minute? I've got something to run past you."

"Sure." Trevor led Jamie into his office and closed the door. "What's up?"

"Here's the thing. I know you've got a lot on your plate right now, with the bar and everything, and it's probably not even fair to talk to you about this, but I want you to come back to Swerve." When Trevor opened his mouth to speak, Jamie put his hand up, cutting him off.

"Hear me out. Not as a bartender but as a consultant."

Trevor blinked. "What?"

"We've talked about this before. But one problem with Swerve that I've been finding lately has been a lack of consistency with the bar service at all of the different locations. The menus are all different, bartenders use different ingredients in set recipes, quality of service—you know I can't have that type of inconsistency. We need to enforce a company-wide standard, so I need someone who knows what they're doing, who knows what it's like behind the bar, to ensure that the standard is being followed."

"Dude, I would love to help you, but I just opened this place."

"I get that. And I know that the timing isn't great for you. But it would only be a part-time gig, with some travel. I just need someone to oversee training of bartenders, managers and mixologists and implementing a new bar menu. I need you. We've created a new role for you *specifically* in the company."

Trevor could tell his friend needed his help, and with everything that Jamie had done for him, Trevor knew that he could spare some time. "What do you need?"

Jamie outlined the details of the position, most notably the high pay and the travel for what would essentially be a part-time job, meaning that Trevor would actually have the time to do it and to also focus on his own business. Trevor nodded. "Yeah, I'll do it."

"Great, awesome. You have no idea what that means to me." Jamie extended his hand and Trevor shook it.

Jamie moved to leave but turned quickly, as if he had just remembered something else. "Oh, yeah, and I have another question to ask you."

"Yeah, and what's that?"

"We've been getting into the whole wedding-planning thing…"

"And how is that going?"

Jamie shrugged. "I try to stay out of the way, but I was told by my beautiful fiancée that I might need a best man."

"Oh, really?" Trevor smiled and crossed his arms over his chest.

"Yeah…" Jamie trailed off and exhaled a puff of breath. "You're really going to make me ask you, aren't you?"

He nodded. "Yeah, probably."

"Want to be my best man?"

"Of course, I will," Trevor said, laughing, and the men hugged. "There's no way I would refuse that." Trevor grinned. "Should we start planning the shower now? I was thinking a brunch…"

"You're an asshole." Jamie pushed his shoulder. "All you have to worry about is the bachelor party and making sure that neither of us is too hungover to stand on my wedding day."

"I think I can handle that." Trevor was serious, but then he laughed. He was more than excited to be able to be there for his best friend on his wedding day. But he felt the room needed a little levity. "I mean, I can probably handle that."

ABBY PASSED THROUGH the threshold of Langered. People were shoulder to shoulder and everyone was having a great time. She looked around for Trevor, but she didn't see him. Instead, she saw Maya wave at her from her spot near the bar.

She hugged her friend. "Have you seen Trevor?"

"Yeah, he and Jamie went into Trevor's office."

Abby looked up in time to see Jamie exit the office alone, smiling. Whatever they had been discussing had gone well, it seemed. She turned to Maya. "Do you mind—"

"Just go," her friend told her with a laugh as Jamie made his way back.

Abby pushed through the crowd and then knocked on the still-closed door of Trevor's office. She opened the door a crack and saw Trevor sitting at his desk, his fingers tented in front of his face, deep in thought. He looked up and smiled when he saw her.

"Hey, mind if I come in?"

"Of course not." He stood, smiling. "I'm glad you made it."

"I wouldn't have missed it. You holding up all right?"

Trevor nodded. "Yeah, it's just a lot to take in tonight with the bar and Jamie just offered me a new position at Swerve and their wedding. And mostly, being with you. There's just a lot of changes."

Abby smiled. "Sure are. So tell me about this job," she said. He gave her the details and she threw her arms around his neck. "That's amazing! Congratulations!" She kissed him. "Everything looks great out there."

Trevor nodded. "Thanks." He frowned and pulled at the collar of his shirt. She knew he hated wearing the suit he had on, even if he looked incredible in the gray three-piece suit, paired with a blue shirt and yellow tie. It wasn't him.

He sat at the desk, still fidgeting with his clothing. Abby laughed and sat on his desk, perching in front of him. Watching her with a sly smile, he stopped and sat back in his chair. He put his hands on her knees and pushed her legs apart. He scooted forward in his wheeled chair, locked his hands around her hips and pulled her to him.

Abby leaned in, took his face between her palms and kissed him. He was hers. She felt his fingers squeeze and knead her ass. She opened her mouth and his tongue entwined and slid against hers...

She pulled away. "Wait a minute."

"What?" Trevor looked just as grateful and disheveled as she felt. His breath was heavy. "What's wrong?"

Abby looked him up and down. "We need to get rid of all of this," she said, laughing, referring to his clothing.

He laughed, as well. She put her hands on the tie, the very same one that she'd used to tie him to his headboard. She gave it a tug, undoing the knot at his neck and pushed his jacket from his shoulders. "Well, now we're talking." He reached around for the zipper of her dress.

"Whoa." She stepped away from his grasp and finished rolling his shirtsleeves up to his elbows. When he pulled her closer and reached for her zipper once again, she had to use all of her restraint not to melt into his arms. "We are not having sex right now."

"No?" He furrowed his brow. "Are you sure? It seemed like we were going to."

"No." Abby giggled at his perturbed expression. She

pointed at the door, beyond which the party continued without them. "You've got a huge party going on out there. This is your night. Go out there. You should be enjoying it."

He looked her up and down, his eyes traveling over her body. She felt the heat of his scrutiny and she almost fell into him. He ran his hands from her hips up her waist to find her breasts. She instinctively leaned into his hands. He moaned. "I know that I would enjoy this a lot more," he said, raising a sexy eyebrow. He kissed her neck.

She sighed. "Well, maybe we can spare a couple of minutes."

"What I want to do to you right now will take a lot more than a couple of minutes."

"Well, I guess that will have to wait until later tonight." She watched his face as she ran her hand lower, opening the fly of his pants, finding him stiff. She extracted him from his boxers and stroked him up and down his length.

He groaned. "But, in the meantime, why don't we christen this office?" His mouth descended upon hers once again, and she was glad she wouldn't have to wait until later that night to feel him. Her arms encircled his neck and he pushed her down on the desk. He lifted her skirt over her hips. She hissed when his fingers traced the lines of her, applying the slightest amount of pressure to her clit. Her back arched, and he kissed her again, before he thrust fully inside her.

She had to stop herself from crying out as she felt him filling her so completely. He pulled out before slamming into her once again. His hips pumped wildly and hers lifted to meet him as she grabbed and clawed at his back.

Abby felt her orgasm rise. "Faster," she begged him.

"You got it," he said, his voice gruff.

Before she could do anything else, she was coming, and she felt the waves wash over her just before Trevor came with his own throaty groan.

Their breathing was interrupted by a curt knock on the door. "Hey, Trev," Jamie called. "It's time for a toast. Come on out."

"Be out in a second," he said hoarsely. He was still buried deep inside her, and as he stood, the movement pushed him, still hard, deeper inside and she sighed.

When he finally withdrew, he tucked himself back into his pants, followed by his shirt. Abby noticed that he ignored the tie and jacket that she had stripped from him. She smiled and stood, as well, straightening her dress over her hips. "Everyone is probably going to know what we did in here," she said as she finger-combed her hair.

"Yeah, probably," he said and laughed, kissing her.

"I've got some news of my own." She smiled at him.

"And what's that?"

"You just made love to the new senior marketing account executive at Bon Temps."

With a whoop, Trevor wrapped his arms around her and hugged her, swinging her around.

"That's fantastic! Congratulations!" He looked around the room and raised an eyebrow. "Do you want to celebrate again?"

"Get out there," she laughed, pushing at his shoulders. "Your well-wishers await."

He started for the door but stopped and quickly

turned toward her. Before she knew it, she was swept up once again in his arms. He kissed her hard, and she didn't think she would ever tire of being kissed by him. She whimpered involuntarily when he let her go. "I can't wait until we can get out of here and I can be with you again," he whispered in her ear, making her shiver in his arms.

Abby wanted nothing more than to feel him all over, inside her, again. "Me, too. But this is your night. Enjoy it."

"I think I will, especially now that that damn tie isn't choking me."

Jamie pounded on the door again.

"You better get out there, hotshot," she said.

"Not without you." He grabbed her hand and pulled her toward the door.

Abby followed, folding up his tie and putting it in her purse. "I can think of a couple of better uses for it. Can't you?"

His eyebrows shot up. "I can. Why don't you come home with me tonight and for the next two thousand nights and you can show me?"

"I'm looking forward to it," she said as they opened the door and joined the party.

* * * * *

#931 SIZZLING SUMMER NIGHTS
Made in Montana • by Debbi Rawlins
Rancher Seth Landers is striving to rebuild his family's
trust and his place in the community. Beautiful visitor
Hannah Hastings has her own agenda. Will she be his
greatest reward...or his biggest downfall?

#932 TEMPTED
by Kimberly Van Meter
Former air force pilot Teagan Carmichael is maneuvered into
going on a singles cruise, where he meets Harper Riley, the
sexiest woman he's ever seen. There's only one problem—
she's a con artist.

#933 HER HOLIDAY FLING
Wild Wedding Nights • by Jennifer Snow
Hayley Hanna needs a fake fiancé for her corporate retreat,
and Chase Hartley is perfect—he's sexy, funny and kind—but
it's just a business deal. That means no kissing, no sex and *no*
falling in love!

#934 A COWBOY IN PARADISE
by Shana Gray
In her designer dress and high-heeled shoes, Jimi clearly
didn't belong on a dusty Hawaiian ranch. Or with rugged
cowboy Dallas Wilde. Dallas may be a delicious temptation,
but could a city girl ever trade Louboutins for lassoes?

REQUEST YOUR FREE BOOKS!
2 FREE NOVELS PLUS 2 FREE GIFTS!

HARLEQUIN®

Blaze®
red-hot reads!

YES! Please send me 2 FREE Harlequin® Blaze® novels and my 2 FREE gifts (gifts are worth about $10). After receiving them, if I don't wish to receive any more books, I can return the shipping statement marked "cancel." If I don't cancel, I will receive 4 brand-new novels every month and be billed just $4.74 per book in the U.S. or $5.21 per book in Canada. That's a savings of at least 14% off the cover price. It's quite a bargain. Shipping and handling is just 50¢ per book in the U.S. and 75¢ per book in Canada.* I understand that accepting the 2 free books and gifts places me under no obligation to buy anything. I can always return a shipment and cancel at any time. Even if I never buy another book, the two free books and gifts are mine to keep forever.

150/350 HDN GH2D

Name	(PLEASE PRINT)	
Address		Apt. #
City	State/Prov.	Zip/Postal Code

Signature (if under 18, a parent or guardian must sign)

Mail to the **Reader Service:**
IN U.S.A.: P.O. Box 1867, Buffalo, NY 14240-1867
IN CANADA: P.O. Box 609, Fort Erie, Ontario L2A 5X3

Want to try two free books from another line?
Call 1-800-873-8635 or visit www.ReaderService.com.

* Terms and prices subject to change without notice. Prices do not include applicable taxes. Sales tax applicable in N.Y. Canadian residents will be charged applicable taxes. Offer not valid in Quebec. This offer is limited to one order per household. Not valid for current subscribers to Harlequin Blaze books. All orders subject to credit approval. Credit or debit balances in a customer's account(s) may be offset by any other outstanding balance owed by or to the customer. Please allow 4 to 6 weeks for delivery. Offer available while quantities last.

Your Privacy—The Reader Service is committed to protecting your privacy. Our Privacy Policy is available online at www.ReaderService.com or upon request from the Reader Service.

We make a portion of our mailing list available to reputable third parties that offer products we believe may interest you. If you prefer that we not exchange your name with third parties, or if you wish to clarify or modify your communication preferences, please visit us at www.ReaderService.com/consumerschoice or write to us at Reader Service Preference Service, P.O. Box 9062, Buffalo, NY 14240-9062. Include your complete name and address.

"I think the best we can hope for is no rocks." Seth nodded to an area where the grass had been flattened.

"This is fine with me," she said, and helped him spread the blanket. "What? No pillows?"

Seth chuckled. "You've lived in Dallas too long."

Crouching, he flattened more of the grass before smoothing the blanket over it. "Here's your pillow, princess."

Hannah laughed. "I was joking," she said, then pinned him with a mock glare. "Princess? Ha. Far from it."

"Come here."

"Don't you mean, come here, please?" She watched a shadow cross his face and realized a cloud had passed over the moon. It made him look a little dangerous, certainly mysterious and too damn sexy. He could've just snapped his fingers and she would've scurried over.

"Please," he said.

She gave a final tug on the blanket, buying herself a few seconds to calm down. "Where do you want me?"

"Right here." He caught her arm and gently pulled her closer, then turned her around and put a hand on her shoulder. "Now, look up. How's this view?"

Hannah felt his heat against her back, the steady presence of his palm cupping her shoulder. "Perfect," she whispered.

His warm breath tickled the side of her neck. He pressed his lips against her skin. "You smell good," he murmured, running his hand down her arm. With his other hand he swept the hair away from her neck. His breath stirred the loose strands at the side of her face.

Hannah was too dizzy to think of one damn thing to say. She saw a pair of eerie, yellowish eyes in the trees, low to the ground. Then a howl split the night. She stifled a shriek, whirled and threw her arms around Seth's neck.

He enfolded her in his strong, muscled arms and held her close. "It's nowhere near us."

"I don't know why it made me jumpy," she said, embarrassed but loving the feel of his hard body flush with hers. "I'm used to coyotes."

"That was a wolf."

Wolf? Did they run from humans or put them on the menu? She leaned back and looked up at him. Before she could question whether or not this was a good idea, Seth lowered his head.

Their lips touched and she was lost in the fog.

Don't miss
SIZZLING SUMMER NIGHTS
by Debbi Rawlins, available March 2017 wherever
Harlequin® Blaze® books and ebooks are sold.

www.Harlequin.com

SPECIAL EXCERPT FROM

HQN™

*Single mom Harper Maclean has two priorities—raising her son
and starting over. Her mysterious new neighbor is charming and
sexy, but Diego Torres asks far too many questions…*

*Enjoy a sneak peek of CALL TO HONOR, the first book in the
new **SEAL BROTHERHOOD** series by Tawny Weber.*

Harper stepped outside and froze.

Diego was in his backyard. Barefoot and shirtless, he wore
what looked like black pajama bottoms. Kicks, turns, chops and
punches flowed in a seamlessly elegant dance.

Shirtless.

She couldn't quite get past that one particular point. But instead
of licking her lips, Harper clenched her fists.

She watched him do some sort of flip, feet in the air and his
body resting on one hand. Muscles rippled, but he wasn't even
breathing hard as he executed an elegant somersault to land feet
first on the grass.

Wow.

He had tattoos.

Again, wow.

He had a cross riding low on his hip and something tribal
circling his biceps.

Who knew tattoos were so sexy?

Harper's mouth went dry. Her libido, eight years in deep freeze,
exploded into lusty flames.

The man was incredible.

Short black hair spiked here and there over a face made for
appreciative sighs. Thick brows arched over deep-set eyes, and he
had a scar on his chin that glowed in the moonlight.

Harper decided that she'd better get the hell out of there.

But just as she turned to go, she spotted Nathan's baseball.

"You looking for the ball?" His words came low and easy like his smile.

"Yes, my son lost it." She eyed the distance between her and the ball. It wasn't far, but she'd have to skirt awfully close to the man.

"Good yard for working out," he said with a nod of approval. He grabbed the ball, then stopped a couple of feet from her.

"I should get that to Nathan." She cleared her throat, tried a smile. "He's very attached to it."

"The kid's a pistol." His eyes were much too intense as he watched her face.

That's when she realized what she must look like. She'd tossed an oversize T-shirt atop her green yoga bra and leggings. Her hair was pulled into a sloppy ponytail, and she wore no makeup.

"Thanks for finding it."

His eyes not leaving hers, he moved closer.

Close enough that his scent—fresh male with a hint of earthy sweat and clean soap—wrapped around her.

Finally, he placed the ball in her outstretched hand. "Everything okay?"

No. Unable to resist, she said, "Why do you ask?"

"I don't like seeing a beautiful woman in a hurry to get away from me." The shadows did nothing to hide the wicked charm of his smile or the hint of sexual heat in his gaze.

It was the same heat Harper felt sizzling deep in her belly.

Thankfully, the tiny voice in her mind still had enough control to scream, "Danger."

"I'm hurrying because I don't like to leave my son inside alone," she managed to say. "Again, thanks for your help."

And with that, she slipped through the hedge before he could say another word. It wasn't until she was inside the house that she realized she was holding her breath.

What's next in store for Harper, Diego and the SEAL Brotherhood? Find out when CALL TO HONOR by New York Times *bestselling author Tawny Weber, goes on sale in February 2017.*

Love the Harlequin book you just read?

Your opinion matters.

Review this book on your favorite book site, review site, blog or your own social media properties and share your opinion with other readers!